THE FAIR
MISS FORTUNE

THE FAIR MISS FORTUNE

D. E. STEVENSON

ISIS

LARGE PRINT

Oxford

First published in Great Britain 2011
by
Greyladies
An imprint of
The Old Children's Bookshelf

Published in Large Print 2012 by ISIS Publishing Ltd.,
7 Centremead, Osney Mead, Oxford OX2 0ES
by arrangement with
Greyladies

The moral right of the author has been asserted

British Library Cataloguing in Publication Data
Stevenson, D. E. (Dorothy Emily), 1892–1973.
The fair Miss Fortune.
1. Large type books.
I. Title
823.9'12–dc23

ISBN 978–0–7531–8948–1 (hb)
ISBN 978–0–7531–8949–8 (pb)

Printed and bound in Great Britain by
T. J. International Ltd., Padstow, Cornwall

PART ONE

CHAPTER
ONE

Captain Charles Weatherby decided that the Prestcotts' new house was rather a joke. It was perched upon the very top of the hill — an oval box, white and shining as a newly iced cake. The roof was flat, the corners were rounded, and it was windowed in all directions to the undulating countryside. The chief impression that the house produced upon its beholder was one of impermanence — it had not been there yesterday, and it might be gone tomorrow — for it appeared to have no roots in the ground. Charles Weatherby decided that with a little imagination one could see it as the ark of a very modern Noah, come to rest during the night upon the crest of an English Ararat.

The garden was still unmade; it was merely a large patch of meadow-grass disfigured by builder's litter. There was no hedge, nor any sort of fence to shut it off from the road, but a perfectly good gate swung between two blocks of concrete which matched the house in snowy whiteness. The young man smiled to himself at the jest of a gate where no fence was — this was the kind of jest which appealed to his sense of humour — and, ignoring a beaten path which skirted the pillar,

Charles Weatherby opened the gate and entered in proper style.

He mounted the gentle slope towards the door, and, as he did so, gradually became aware of a buzzing sound like a swarm of giant bees gathering honey in a lavender bush. The sound grew louder as he approached until it resembled the din which emanates from the monkey house at the Zoo, but Charles was well aware that it was neither bees nor monkeys but merely the Prestcotts' house-warming sherry-party in full swing.

Charles frowned. He had not wanted to come to this party, and, now that he was almost there, he wanted to even less, but his mother had made him accept the invitation, saying that it would be "so nice" for him "to meet all his old friends after being away in India all these years." Charles was quite sure that it would not be nice, for he was shy with the shyness which besets the exile when he returns to his native place. He had been abroad for three years — no more — but he was convinced that these people would not want him; that they would have forgotten him; that they would find him awkward and gauche, his clothes old-fashioned and shabby, his manners strange. He felt that it would have been easier to meet these people one by one, casually, in the village, or on the golf course; he felt that to plunge right into the whole crowd jabbering together in an over-heated room was going to take the kind of courage he did not possess. Put him at the head of his Gurkhas, and he would lead them against the savage hordes of the North West Frontier, or ask him to hold an outpost and he would hold it to the last man.

Charles had tried to explain all this to Mrs. Weatherby, but without much avail. "Of course they haven't forgotten you," she declared firmly. "They often talk about you, and your best suit looks very nice indeed. Besides," she had added, with a twinkle in her eye, "besides, I do want to know what the new house is like, and what everybody is saying about it."

He had known, then, that there was no escape, he must drink this cup to the bitter dregs — and bitter the dregs would be if he knew anything of Mrs. Prestcott's sherry.

Mrs. Weatherby was an invalid, so she could not go to the party herself, and, though Charles would have preferred to serve her in some other, less heroic, way, he knew that, if she really wanted him to go, then go he must. He sighed, "Very well then," he said, and answered the invitation in the glowing affirmative language that convention dictated.

Mrs. Weatherby had known that she could make him go, but she was pleased to have accomplished her end so easily. She was not a foolish woman, nor was she so dense that she could not understand and sympathise with her son's feelings, but it had always been her belief that if you intend to take a cold bath it is better to jump in quickly rather than immerse your shivering limbs in the icy water bit by bit. She wanted Charles to enjoy his leave, to go about and meet everybody and play golf, and she was convinced that the sooner he started the better it would be.

Charles Weatherby was now standing upon the semicircular concrete doorstep of the brand-new house and admiring the magnificent view. To his left was the Dingleford Golf Course, spread out upon the undulating hills like a bright green cloth; it was ringed with heath and pine trees and dotted with yellow bunkers. In a gentle hollow at the farther end of the course lay the pond, gleaming placidly in the summer sunshine, it looked very innocent and friendly but in reality it was neither, and Charles was fully aware that deep in its calm and kindly-seeming bosom it harboured hundreds of perfectly good golf-balls, the price that every golfer must pay for a slice at the thirteenth tee. In front of Charles, below him on the hill, were several pleasant houses with gardens and trees (his mother's house was one of them, the smallest, but perhaps the prettiest of all) and at the bottom of the hill was the village of Dingleford spread out before him like a map. There was the grey stone church, with its Norman tower, flanked by an oblong building with a pointed roof which he knew to be the vicarage, and beyond that was the village green, a triangular patch of verdant sward shaded by fine old trees.

At the other side of the green lay the Inn — the Cat and Fiddle — with its huddle of dilapidated roofs which had once been posting stables. "I must drop in and see Widgett," said Charles to himself, for Widgett was a very old friend and a tremendous "character". He knew all the local gossip, could tip you a certain winner and was a gold-mine of funny stories; and besides all this he could draw you a pint of the best ale to be found in England. Yes, Widgett must certainly be seen and heard, and his wares sampled before Charles was many days older.

On Charles' right the country rolled away to the skyline, with fields and trees and tiny grey-roofed farms, and winding in and out he could see the Dingle — a stream justly celebrated for its trout. Charles followed the course of the stream, saw how it slid past the village where the old ford was, and curled away southwards towards the sea. About half a mile below the village there was a thick clump of trees, and here lay the Prestcotts' old house with nothing visible save its chimney stacks. Charles knew the house well, for he and Harold Prestcott had been inseparable companions in the old days. They had climbed trees, fished the Dingle, and got into all the usual sort of scrapes. The Prestcotts' old house was very old indeed, a damp uncomfortable place with uneven floors and latticed windows; there were unexpected steps in the darkest corners, and oaken beams which hit you on the head when you weren't looking. Charles could not help smiling to himself at the contrast between Mrs. Prestcott's old house and the new one which she had caused to be built. She was the kind of woman whose own possessions are perfect in her sight, and she had been positively lyrical over the charms of her "Elizabethan Cottage." What, Charles wondered, would she have to say about the amenities of her cardboard box.

CHAPTER
TWO

It was very pleasant to linger thus upon the doorstep and revive his memories of his native place, and Charles could have lingered here for a good hour if it had not been that he was already overdue at the sherry-party. He turned his back upon Dingleford with a little sigh, and was about to ring the bell, when the door was flung open and a young man appeared upon the threshold — it was Harold Prestcott himself.

"Charles!" he cried delightedly. "So you've come! I was beginning to think you'd funked it. Have you been waiting ages? I suppose everyone was too busy to answer the bell — why on earth didn't you walk in?"

It was difficult in the circumstances to find any suitable reply and Charles was still searching for one when his friend continued: "I was just crossing the hall and saw your shadow on the glass door. Come along in, old fellow, how are you? Doesn't it seem ages since we've seen each other?"

It did seem ages. They shook hands in the slightly embarrassed manner of two young Britishers who like each other but have not met for years. Life had torn them apart, and dealt with them so differently that they were strangers to each other's thoughts, and it was doubtful whether they would be able to find any mutual interests to bring them together again. In appearance they were entirely different. Charles Weatherby was tall and lean and bronzed, with fair straight hair brushed backwards from his broad brow. His expression was somewhat stern as befitted a man who was used to command and who carried the responsibilities of his calling, but when he smiled the sternness vanished, the bright blue eyes twinkled pleasantly and the white teeth flashed. Harold Prestcott was shorter than Charles by several inches. He looked much younger than his age, for his face was round and smooth, and his brown eyes were soft and appealing. His dark brown hair was slightly wavy and he wore it parted at the side.

The two young men took stock of each other with sidelong glances as Charles hung up his hat. Harold was exactly the same as when he was a boy, thought Charles. He had grown larger, that was all, and if he didn't watch it he would begin to put on weight. Harold's summing up was more admiring and less critical — how he envied that tall lean body and that firm brown face.

"Come on, hurry up," he said smilingly, as Charles dawdled over the exact disposal of his hat. "You know everybody here, so you needn't be shy."

"That's just the reason —" Charles began, but he had no time to finish his complaint, for Harold had opened the door and was ushering him in.

★   ★   ★

The room was full of bright glaring sunshine, and of people drinking sherry and eating biscuits and sandwiches, and sausages on little sticks. They were much too busy talking to worry about Charles, and for this mercy he was absurdly thankful. He spotted his hostess near the window and edged his way round the room with the laudable intention of greeting her as a good guest should. Several people spoke to him casually as he passed, ("Hullo, Charles, back again?" they enquired, and Charles smiled and agreed that he was), but on the whole his arrival caused singularly little notice, and the experience was not half so bad as he had feared. He waited until Mrs. Prestcott should have finished her conversation and turn to speak to him, and all at once he realised the odd fact that he liked these people individually — it was only *en masse* that he detested them. When people got together like this, thought Charles, they suddenly became like caricatures — for instance Miss Ames' long nose grew an eighth of an inch longer as she jabbered so earnestly to Mr. Manley; her hair receded more than ever from her high bumpy forehead, and her halo hat slid slightly to one side. If Miss Ames had walked onto the stage at a music hall she would have brought down the house. Mr. Manley, desiccated already, took on the appearance of a prune, so small and wizened and dry was he that one could scarcely believe that he harboured any liquid in his veins. It was the same with everybody here; they lost their humanity, grew gargoylish, or assumed the likeness of animals. Colonel Staunton was exactly like a pig — it was something about the way his chin and nose poked forward from his thick neck, and the way his forehead receded; something about his little twinkling eyes, knowing, lewd, and a trifle greedy; something about the smooth tight pinkness of his skin and the sparseness of his tufty white hair. He was a nice pig, of course — and exceedingly clean — Charles had always liked Colonel Staunton.

At this moment Mrs. Prestcott interrupted her conversation to give Charles her long thin hand — it was as clammy and boneless as a filleted sole. "Dear Charles," she murmured, "so nice of you to come! You know everybody don't you?" and then, continuing her previous conversation, she declared:

"Of course not, my dear Mrs. Manley, I should never have thought of leaving Dingleford Cottage if it had not been for The Road."

"So sad for you!" agreed Mrs. Manley regretfully.

"It was a wrench, but now that it is a *fait accompli* I am quite glad. One should move with the times."

"How right you are!" exclaimed Mrs. Manley more cheerfully.

"I think so — yes, I believe I am right. One should not look backwards, nor rebel against the inevitable. Harold and I were very happy together in our dear little cottage, buried from the world, but there is no reason why we should not be happy here. I had no choice but to move when The Road started."

"The Road" — Charles heard it mentioned on all sides as he squeezed his way to a side table and procured some refreshments. He knew all about this road, of course, (for his mother had kept him well posted in the Dingleford news) but he had not realised that it had caused such heartburnings among the residents. He remembered now that an arterial road was being built between the two large towns of Horbury and Billington, and that it had been planned to run straight across country, about half a mile south of the village of Dingleford. How are these things settled, Charles wondered, and who is the man that decides their course. Perhaps some clerk in a government department provides himself with a map and a ruler and draws a straight line between the two points. Charles liked to play with this absurd idea, visualising as the *Deus ex Machina*, a small man with pince-nez perched on the tip of his pointed nose; a man with sandy hair, a conscientious nature and a large family. The next stage of the Road is a Bill in Parliament — everybody knows that — and, if its course happens to interfere with the amenities of Somebody-High-Up, so many obstacles are discovered that the little man's map, bandied about from office to office and from hand to hand, becomes dog-eared and dirty, and is finally put away, together with a sheaf of acrid correspondence upon the subject, on the highest shelf of the office from which it emanated.

It was not thus, however, with the Horbury-Billington Bypass, for nobody had minded much whether it got through Parliament or not — Nobody who was Anybody. Mrs. Prestcott had minded a good deal when she had discovered that it would cut through her garden not thirty yards from her Elizabethan Cottage, but Mrs. Prestcott did not count. She pulled every string she could lay hands on without avail and at last she realised that the only thing to be done was to get as much compensation as possible and retire from the unequal contest with her flags flying. All this had happened some time ago, and Mrs. Prestcott's retirement was complete. The Road was nearly finished and it only remained for the bridge to be built — the bridge which was to carry it over the Dingle and join the two ribbons of tar macadam into one long straight stretch from Billington to Horbury.

The residents of Dingleford had evidently got this road on their nerves. "Buses, of course!" Miss Ames was saying, shaking her head so regretfully that the halo hat slid even further over her left ear. "And trippers on Sundays," put in Colonel Staunton, "picnicking on the Village Green."

"But, Sir," began Charles, trying to alleviate this gloom. "But, Sir, they'll go straight through, won't they? I mean you won't be able to see the village from the road. What would bring trippers to Dingleford?"

"What brings them anywhere?" boomed the Colonel. "Mark my words the whole Green will be strewn with orange skins and paper bags. Why only the other day —"

"I'm afraid you're right, Colonel," Mr. Manley declared. "Yes, I'm afraid you're right. Our village is a little bit of the past, peaceful and unspoilt by the march of so-called civilisation. The church with its Norman tower; the Green itself with its Elizabethan Well, and its fine old trees —"

"How brave and good Mrs. Prestcott is!" exclaimed Mrs. Manley, who had suddenly joined the group. "Such wonderful resignation! I think it was too dreadful to be turned out of her lovely cottage —"

"What can't be cured must be endured," observed Mr. Ames.

"Endured! *She* needn't complain," declared the Colonel roundly. "I don't mind betting she got a good sum in compensation for her amenities — and the place was as damp and dark as the grave."

CHAPTER
THREE

Charles was listening to the conversation and sipping the amber liquid which Mrs. Prestcott had provided for her guests when a silvery voice in his ear enquired softly, "And what does our little Charles think of the chimpanzees' tea party?"

He swung round quickly and saw Erica Manley, smiling at him from beneath the brim of a bright green hat. Only one eye was visible to Charles, but it was as full of mischief as any two eyes have a right to be. He could also see, beneath the dipping brim, half a nose, one cheek, and a pair of scarlet lips.

"Erica!" he exclaimed. "How nice to see you."

"I've been watching you for some time," she declared, "but you were lost to the world. Our Brave Bronzed Soldier Recently Returned from the Outposts of Empire, Surveys the Festive Scene with a Supercilious Air."

"I wasn't," said Charles gravely. "At least I didn't mean to —"

Erica laughed. "I don't blame you — far from it," she declared. "Come on, Charles, let's get out of this. I want to talk to you."

Charles was only too delighted to escape from the noise and the heat of the overcrowded room, he followed her into the hall, and up the polished wooden stairs, uncarpeted in the fashion of the moment. The more he saw of the house the more it amazed him — it was so dazzlingly bright, so bare, such a rainbow of crude colours. Erica led him across a landing and up another flight of stairs and presently they emerged upon a flat roof which stretched the whole length of the building. It was rather a pleasant place and was obviously used a good deal by the Prestcotts, for it was furnished with flowering plants in boxes, a few deck chairs, and an enormous sun umbrella of gaily striped twill.

"It's rather fun, isn't it?" Erica said, as she dropped into a deck chair and stretched out her silk-clad legs. "There's a good deal about the house I can't bear, but I *do* like the roof. Ma Prestcott and Harold do their sunbathing up here — but *not* in the nude, of course."

"You seem to know all about the house," Charles declared, as he sat down in the patch of shade beneath the striped umbrella.

"Yes, are you surprised?"

"I am a little," he admitted smiling.

"I suppose you didn't think I liked Ma Prestcott enough to be free of her house," declared Erica maliciously.

It was exactly what he had thought, but it sounded unpleasant put like this — unnecessarily unpleasant.

"I don't like Ma Prestcott," she continued. "Who could? But Harold is rather sweet, really, with his doggy eyes — poor, poor Harold! No, Charles, I've got no designs upon Harold — definitely not — I'm just frightening Ma Prestcott a little, for her own good . . . and Harold's good . . . and because I haven't got anything better to do. Ma Prestcott is *so* worried, the poor thing doesn't know what she wants. On the one hand I'm a good match, you see — lots of money and all that — but on the other hand she wants to keep dear little Harold tied to her apron strings."

"Why on earth are you telling me all this?" asked Charles uncomfortably.

"Why not?" enquired Erica, stretching her arms and yawning. "I must talk to somebody, mustn't I?"

Charles did not know what to say, and there was silence for a moment or two. He had been more than a little in love with Erica the last time he was home on leave, but he had stifled his feelings and departed without a word. As a subaltern in the Indian Army with nothing beyond his pay he believed that he had no right to speak of love to Erica Manley. He would not have hesitated to ask a poor woman to share his comparative poverty, but he was too independent to want a rich wife. Erica was young and pretty, and she had several other young men dancing attendance upon her, so Charles withdrew as gracefully as he could. He was certainly more than a little in love, for he had cut her picture out of the *Tatler* and framed it — smiling to himself somewhat wryly at his foolishness. The picture had stood on his dressing-table for months, had stood there, in fact, until it had got lost when the Battalion had moved to Summer Camp. Now here was Erica again, and here was he, but the thrill and the glamour of her presence was gone. That seemed very odd to Charles.

"I suppose you think it dreadful of me to talk like this," said Erica suddenly, casting off her feigned languor and sitting bolt upright in the deck chair. "Why don't you say so straight out, Charles? Plain speaking is what I like — plain speaking — not this eternal yatter of inanities. Sometimes I feel as if I should burst! Heavens, what a dull hole this is!"

"Perhaps the road will liven it up a bit," Charles suggested.

"The Road!" she cried, "I'm sick of the Road! I wish it was going straight through this beastly village! That would make them sit up! I wish thousands of trippers would come and camp on the green — how I should laugh! It would be something to see, at least. There would be some life about the place. Why do they want to keep Dingleford like this — dull — deadly — quiet? Because they're all half-dead themselves, that's why."

"Couldn't you get away for a bit, if you feel like this?"

"That's what I want — to get away — anywhere. But Father won't let me go, won't let me have a penny. Oh it's so unfair, so absolutely Victorian. Sometimes I feel I can't bear it a moment longer."

Charles lay back and looked at the sky. He could not look at Erica for she had embarrassed him by her wild outburst.

She had been letting off steam, and perhaps it had been good for her to do so, but it was very

18

uncomfortable for him. Had he made a mistake about Erica, he wondered. Should he have spoken to her three years ago and given her the chance of a fuller if less comfortable life? Was it too late now?

"You're very serious," she said at last in a lighter tone.

"You mean dull," replied Charles gravely, "as dull as Dingleford."

"So it seems," she agreed.

"I'm sorry, Erica," he cried impulsively. "Perhaps we could think of something — Perhaps something will turn up —"

"Perhaps something won't," said Erica bitterly. She rose and leant on the parapet, gazing out on the sunlit country with unseeing eyes.

When Charles and Erica returned to the drawing-room they found it a good deal less crowded, for some of the guests had gone, and Charles was aware that several people had noted their absence and their return.

Mrs. Prestcott bore down upon them from the other side of the room.

"We must have a little chat, dear Charles," she cooed. "I've been so busy seeing that everyone was happy. How is Mother? So brave and cheerful, I always think."

Charles winced at the words. It was true that his Mother was brave and cheerful, but her courage was sacred to him and not to be spoken of lightly and airily by such as Mrs. Prestcott.

"Mother's all right," he said shortly. "She sent her love."

"Sweet of her!" declared Mrs. Prestcott. "I must come and see her soon. We have been *so* busy moving that I haven't had a moment. What do you think of the house? Did Erica show it to you? . . . Naughty puss, I wanted to take you round myself."

"It's very gay."

"Yes, isn't it? All those bright colours are so amusing, and so — so bracing. Harold and I are like babies over our new toy."

Beneath this rattle of musketry Charles was aware that the dark eyes of his hostess were probing him remorselessly, and he suddenly realised that Mrs. Prestcott was not really foolish as he had always supposed. She was not a vapid gasbag, but a scheming woman, perhaps even a dangerous one. He also saw — or thought he saw — that she was pleased to see him with Erica Manley. Was this because she hoped that he would draw Erica away from Harold? Charles thought it was, and he was further strengthened in his conviction when she continued in dulcet tones, "Come and see us often Charles, won't you? Harold and I have been looking forward to your leave — you'll find us just the same as ever in spite of our new surroundings . . . or will you?" she questioned, laughing a little at the absurd thought. "Perhaps we shall change. We seem to have stepped out of the Sixteenth century into the middle of the Twentieth. That's how I see it."

Charles had seen it like that too.

20

"Already we have discovered something new about ourselves — Harold and I," she went on, patting him affectionately on the arm. "Shall I tell you what we have discovered?"

"Er — yes, if you like," agreed Charles, with reluctance. He was convinced that Mrs. Prestcott could have discovered nothing very pleasant about herself, and had no wish to be her Father Confessor.

"We are sun-worshippers," declared Mrs. Prestcott dramatically. "There now, what do you think of that? Yes, we simply worship the sun — so warm and golden and life-giving. And this is our temple," she continued, waving her arms, "our temple to Apollo — the sun god."

"Your temple!" echoed Charles in bewilderment.

"This house," she explained. "The whole house is designed so that every room shall get the maximum of sunlight. The architect was very clever about it. Of course, we haven't actually called it that," she added confidentially. "We've just called it 'Suntrap'."

"Such a sweet name!" declared Mrs. Manley, who had approached to say good-bye.

Colonel Staunton was just behind her, and now he too came forward with outstretched hand. "Good-bye Mrs. Prestcott," he boomed politely. "Good-bye . . . such a pleasant party . . . most enjoyable . . . lovely house . . . fine view."

"So glad you like it," Mrs. Prestcott purred.

"By the way, talking of views," continued the Colonel, pausing at the door. "Have you put a caretaker in Dingleford Cottage? I saw smoke coming from the chimneys down there among the trees."

"I've sold my dear little cottage."

"What? Sold it!" cried the Colonel in amazement. "Who's bought it — eh?"

By this time several other guests had come to make their adieux, and were listening to the conversation with interest. The arrival of a newcomer in Dingleford was News (with a capital N); it affected everybody profoundly. Mrs. Prestcott was somewhat annoyed, for she had intended to keep the whole thing a secret, and to burst her bomb on Dingleford in her own good time, when certain arrangements had been completed and the new owner of the cottage properly installed. She reflected bitterly that it was no use trying to keep anything dark in Dingleford — such nosey parkers they all were!

"It's a young girl called Jane Fortune," said Mrs. Prestcott reluctantly, and then, realising that as the cat was now out of the bag, she had better make the best of it, she smiled sweetly and added: "Such a nice little thing, very pretty and ladylike. I'm sure you'll all be charmed with her."

"How will she like The Road at her back door?" enquired the Colonel bluntly.

"Oh, that's just the idea!" replied his hostess laughing gaily. "That's the whole object, you see. She's going to run a little tea-shop."

"A tea-shop!" cried Mrs. Ruff, the vicar's wife, in dismay.

"Oh, Mrs. Prestcott — your dear little house —" bleated Mrs. Manley.

"One must move with the times," said Mrs. Prestcott. "Lots of people run tea-shops nowadays. This girl is quite a lady but reduced in means — so sad really! I was glad to let her have my dear little house for an old song."

"Humph!" snorted Colonel Staunton incredulously.

"I do hope everyone will be kind to her!" sighed the altruistic lady.

"You don't mean that we are to call!" cried Mrs. Manley in horror-stricken tones.

"Not if you don't want to, of course. I don't want to persuade you to do anything . . . I only feel that this young girl . . . coming to live amongst us . . . surely it would be neighbourly . . . but never mind."

"Well of course —" began Mrs. Manley doubtfully.

"She's just a child, so excited about this New Venture. She and her old nurse — quite a character, I believe — are going to run the tea-shop together and make all the cakes themselves. I do hope they will be successful. We must go and have tea there when it opens — all of us — but of course it isn't nearly ready yet. In fact she is only moving in today. I happen to know this," she added confidentially, "because I asked her to come to my party and she sent me a charming note explaining why she couldn't manage it. I thought the poor little thing could have met us all and got to know us."

"Such a treat for the poor little thing!" whispered Erica, in Charles' ear. "Better than a visit to the Zoo any day."

"What is she like to look at?" Colonel Staunton wanted to know — he was always ready to be kind to a nice-looking young female.

Mrs. Prestcott considered this thoughtfully. "She's a pretty little thing . . . rather unusual somehow . . . small and slight, with very fair hair and dark brown eye-brows. Grey eyes, I think . . . yes . . . grey, with long dark lashes — a bright little creature with plenty to say for herself."

This description of the charms of the fair Miss Fortune affected its hearers in different ways. It left Charles cold, for he had no use for bright little creatures no matter how long their eyelashes might be. Colonel Staunton, on the other hand, was considerably intrigued, and began to wonder how he could approach the young lady. Must he leave the meeting to chance, or could he call and offer to be of service to her — a stranger in a strange land? Miss Ames, who was secretary of the Dingleford Ladies' Golf Club, lost all interest in the newcomer, deciding regretfully that it did not sound as if she would be good enough to play for the Club — pretty girls are seldom good at golf — but Mrs. Manley thought she sounded sweet, and Mrs. Ruff conceived the idea that Miss Fortune would be a great asset to the Woman's Rural Institute where bright little creatures with plenty to say for themselves were worth their weight in gold.

CHAPTER
FOUR

Emma Weatherby was playing patience. It was a very complicated patience played with four packs of cards and Charles had made her a special board, covered with green baize, so that she could lay it out in comfort. Emma liked this game for she found that it helped her to sort out her thoughts. She had so many thoughts — far too many, really — but how could you help thinking too much when you couldn't go about like other people? Emma was deeply concerned with other people's problems and troubles as well as her own, she was benevolently minded. Today the patience was very stubborn; first she was blocked by knaves and then they all got covered and she was stuck for the want of one. It was at this moment that Charles returned from the party. He came over to the sofa and surveyed the game.

"Look, isn't it a bother?" Emma said. "I had dozens of knaves a moment ago."

"It's the queen that's blocking you," Charles pointed out. "That black queen . . . she's like Mrs. Prestcott, isn't she? The same sly scheming look, the same dead-white skin — horrible."

He spoke with such unusual ferocity that Emma was quite startled. "Charles!" she cried.

"Look," he continued, pointing with the stem of his pipe. "Mrs. P. is sitting on the knave of hearts — that's Harold of course — move her into the space and put Harold on top of her . . . see . . . now you've released another knave."

His mother carried out the movement half-heartedly. "But Charles," she said, "what on earth do you mean about Sylvia Prestcott?"

"I don't know," replied Charles thoughtfully. "I just don't like her — that's all. Her hands are clammy."

Emma Weatherby laughed. "Poor Sylvia!" she said.

"You don't like her either, do you?" Charles enquired.

"She isn't exactly my . . . my cup of tea," replied Emma, smiling at the slang phrase which seemed to describe her feelings so exactly. "I saw a lot of her at one time, of course, but that was because circumstances drew us together. We were both widows, and you two boys were friends — these things make ties, especially in a place like this where one's choice is so limited."

"I always thought she was stupid," he said, "but she isn't stupid at all — she's clever."

"Oh — *clever!*"

"You don't think so."

"She's clever enough to be stupid," Emma declared somewhat enigmatically. "Clever enough to know what she wants and to hold on to it tightly, but not clever enough to know that grabbing is never any good in the long run."

Charles considered this. He understood a good deal that was not said. "Harold won't escape," he declared at last, putting his finger on the spot with unerring exactitude.

"I have you far more safely."

"So you're far more clever," he teased.

"Of course, that goes without saying," she agreed. She had been playing out her patience as they talked, for the one movement had started others, and she now saw that with care and forethought the whole thing might work out. She was not really a superstitious woman, but somehow this patience had got muddled up with life, and it seemed important that it should work out smoothly to the end. She had two queens of hearts now, and two knaves — one for each. The knaves were Charles and Harold, but who were the queens?

Charles sat down and began to fill his pipe.

"Did you hate it dreadfully?" she enquired. "Did you hate me for making you go? I've been thinking about you all the time and wondering what you were doing."

"Drinking sherry of course," said Charles, "or at least drinking what Mrs. Prestcott buys from the grocer, and eating congealed sausages — but never mind, it's over now and I've got lots of gossip for you."

"Is it horrid of me to like gossip?"

"No," said Charles thoughtfully. "Why should it be horrid? You don't like unkind gossip, do you?"

Emma considered this. "I'm afraid I like all kinds," she said at last quite seriously. "I like anything about people — people interest me so."

Charles laughed and began to tell his mother about the party.

It was an old habit of theirs that Charles should tell her "all his adventures." He could remember telling her the minute details of his first cricket match which had taken place when he was about nine, and he could remember coming home from school and retailing the history of the term. Charles liked feeling that he could give her this pleasure, and he knew that it *was* a pleasure. Whatever he told her and however long he took about it, Emma was never bored. She had said to him once in a rare moment of rebellion: "What a rotten mother you have got! — no use to anyone!" and Charles had replied fiercely: "You mustn't say that again, you mustn't *think* it. Other chaps' mothers have no time to *listen*." Mrs. Weatherby was comforted. She had all the time there was to listen to Charles.

So Charles told his mother all about the party, he even told her about his conversation with Erica — not all of it, of course — and they discussed Erica's troubles at length. Mrs. Weatherby had been aware of her son's penchant for Erica and had half hoped and half feared that it might "come to something". She wanted Charles to marry, but she was not at all sure that Erica was the right girl. She saw now that Charles had completely recovered from Erica, for no man would thus discuss the future of his beloved.

"Well, don't let's worry about her," said Charles at last. "We can't do anything . . . she'll worstle through somehow, I suppose."

"I wish we could do something about Harold," Emma Weatherby said with a sigh. "Sylvia doesn't let him call his soul his own — it's dreadful really.

Couldn't you do something about it now that you're home?"

"What could I do?"

"Anything!" cried Emma vigorously. "Drag him out to play golf, tell him naughty stories, take him up to London and make him tight —"

Charles gazed at her for a moment, and then roared with laughter. "You're priceless!" he declared. "Can you see Harold and me setting off to London together with the fixed intention of getting tight?"

"No," she admitted, smiling a little, "but it would do him good all the same."

There was no more to be said about the matter, so they abandoned Harold to his fate. The patience was finished now; it had all worked out beautifully — sixteen kings sat smugly upon the top of their neat little packs of cards. Emma sighed with satisfaction and lay back on her cushions. "Tell me about the new house," she commanded.

Charles was quite ready to comply. He told her all about it in great detail, and he told her how it was really a Temple to Apollo, the Sun God. Emma laughed inordinately at the idea.

"They're bound to change," she decided. "All animals do if you take them out of the shade into the sunlight — all animals and plants. I shouldn't wonder if poor Harold were to grow up and astonish Sylvia — wouldn't that be fun?"

Charles agreed that it would. "By the by, had you heard that she had sold the cottage?" he enquired.

"No!" cried Emma incredulously. "Has she really? How exciting! Did she tell you who's bought it?"

"It's a Miss Fortune —" Charles began.

"A misfortune!"

"Yes."

"How can it be a misfortune? Who said it was?"

"Mrs. Prestcott told me herself."

"Told you it was a misfortune?"

"Yes."

"Sylvia must be mad," declared Mrs. Weatherby firmly.

"Why . . . how . . . what do you know about it?" asked Charles in a bewildered tone.

"I don't know anything," his mother replied, "except that Sylvia is extremely lucky to have sold the cottage at any price . . . that damp, dark hole . . ."

"I know," Charles agreed.

"Then why say it's a misfortune?"

"Because it is," cried Charles, beginning to laugh. "Oh mother . . . that's her name."

"What's her name?"

"MISS FORTUNE."

"Oh, I see," said Emma smiling. "Goodness, the woman must be tired of jokes about her name, mustn't she? I wonder what she's like."

Charles knew exactly what she was like. He enumerated Miss Fortune's charms in the Prestcott manner, and did it so well that his mother laughed inordinately again.

"But the girl is probably quite nice all the same," declared Emma, wiping her eyes. "Poor thing, buried in

30

that horrid dark cottage, with no electric light or anything! Charles, don't you think you might go down there tomorrow morning and bring her back to lunch?"

"I might," agreed Charles with scant enthusiasm.

A quarter of a mile away, and a hundred feet nearer the heavens, another widow and her son were holding a postmortem on the party. They were holding it in the morning-room whence they had fled from the horrible remains of the feast. Sylvia Prestcott was lying on the sofa, her long thin legs stretched out in graceful ease; Harold was sitting on a stool beside her; on the floor at his feet squatted Francesca, a black pedigree pug, who was the joy of Sylvia's life and the bane of Harold's; and between them stood a large box of chocolate creams, a delicacy to which all three were extremely partial.

"Charles is ageing rapidly," Mrs. Prestcott declared. "So haggard and lined — nobody would think he was only twenty-eight. He looks years older than you."

"I thought he looked brown and fit," said Harold with unusual temerity.

"Yellow," said Sylvia firmly. "He probably drinks too much. Did you see how Erica made a dead set at him. She doesn't mean to let him escape this time . . . I can't think what she sees in him, can you?"

"She was just being kind —"

"Kind? Have you ever seen a cat being kind to a mouse? She's got her claws into him . . . it will be amusing to watch the fun."

Harold swallowed nervously. He wanted to find something to say in defence of his friends, but the words would not come.

"Mr. Manley was more prosy than ever, and Mrs. Manley as silly as usual," continued their late hostess vindictively. "She couldn't be sillier if she tried: 'Oh Mrs. Prestcott, your dear little house!'"

Harold smiled, for his mother had caught the bleating tone of her victim so exactly, besides Harold had not much use for Mrs. Manley himself — she was a tiresome woman at the best of times.

"They were all annoyed about the tea-shop, weren't they?" he said.

"Yes, I knew they would be annoyed," Sylvia declared stretching out her hand for a chocolate cream and selecting one with a crystallised violet on the top. "I knew they'd all be furious, but why should I care? If I hadn't sold it to that Fortune girl I shouldn't have sold it at all. Nobody wants to live on the edge of an arterial road."

Harold agreed. He helped himself to a cream, and gave one to Francesca who slobbered and snuffled over it with rapturous greed.

"I wonder if it will pay," he said.

"It's extremely doubtful," declared Sylvia, "but I've got the money, anyhow."

Harold did not answer. He was so used to his mother's selfishness and ruthlessness that he took her attitude as a matter of course. Her malice did not shock him unless it was directed against his own particular friends and even then he was too completely under her

32

thumb to make more than a feeble protest. Harold's nature was pliable, and Sylvia had bent him into the shape she desired. She had never allowed him to go to school, saying that he was too delicate for the rough and tumble life. When he had wanted to try for the Navy she had put him off with smiles and promises until it was too late. After that Harold had turned his thoughts towards engineering as a profession, but had met with so little encouragement that his enthusiasm had died a natural death. Harold was delicate — that was the excuse. "Nothing really wrong, you know, but he needs a mother's care."

Harold had had "a mother's care" all his life, he was hers, body and soul.

"Are you going to call on Miss Fortune?" enquired Harold idly.

"Yes," said Sylvia, "yes, I shall call — just to show Mrs. Manley that she can't dictate to me. We needn't bother much about the girl," she added amiably, "but I shall certainly call."

There was a little silence and then she continued: "That dreadful Mr. Ames! Did you speak to him, Harold? He goes about dripping platitudes — so tiresome — and his sister is almost worse — last year's halo hat over one ear — as for Colonel Staunton, he gets more unbearable every day."

"Still it was a great success," said Harold complacently, and he helped himself to another chocolate cream.

CHAPTER
FIVE

Charles had bought a small second-hand car to run while he was on leave, but he knew very little about cars and had begun to entertain the horrible suspicion that he had been "done". Edgar had a very peculiar temperament, some days he would go like mad and delight his owner's heart, but other days he sulked and would scarcely go at all. Charles went out to the garage the morning after the party and unlocked the double doors. He looked at Edgar thoughtfully, and it seemed to him that Edgar stared back in an extremely human way.

"Come up, old chap!" Charles adjured him. "We're going to see a pretty girl today — the fair Miss Fortune — you'll enjoy that, won't you?"

Edgar looked far from pleased. There was something about the tilt of his headlamps that Charles didn't like at all. If Edgar had been a mule Charles would have known exactly how to tackle this wicked look of his, but unfortunately Edgar was not a mule. He refused to start with the self-starter and Charles was obliged to find the handle, and crank for dear life. It was a job he detested, and he was very hot and bothered before Edgar sprang into a reluctant buzz.

Charles left Edgar buzzing and went back to the house to wash his hands. He looked into his Mother's room and grinned at her from the door.

"Edgar's sulky this morning," announced Charles. "He doesn't like women."

"The brute!" exclaimed Mrs. Weatherby vigorously.

"So don't worry if we're late for lunch — it will be Edgar's fault."

"Charles, come here," Emma said, raising herself in bed and looking at him critically. "Charles — oh Charles, I thought so! Why haven't you put on a decent suit?"

Like a small boy detected in mischief Charles wriggled at the door. "Really Mother . . . supposing I have words with Edgar on the way? Damn it all, I can't crawl under the brute in my best suit."

"You can't call on Miss Fortune in Khaki drill slacks —"

"Why not?"

"— and look at the oil on your sleeve — you're incorrigible!"

"If Miss Fortune doesn't like me in my old clothes —" he began — "And anyhow," he added incoherently, "you'd never have known *what* I had on if I hadn't had the decency to look in and see you."

"Now I ask you — what has that got to do with it?" cried Emma. "I've seen you, and you're a positive disgrace. They say women are illogical, but —"

He was gone. She heard him running down the stairs. What a boy he was — and yet he was a man, a real man. Emma was lucky in her son and some woman would be lucky in her husband. If only she lets me keep a little bit of him, thought Emma, I shan't grab, I shan't even hold on, for that's the way to lose everything.

Meanwhile Charles and Edgar were buzzing down to Dingleford Cottage to see Miss Fortune. They passed through the village, and along the road by the Dingle. This road was in very bad repair for Mrs. Prestcott had not mended it since she had decided to move. There were deep ruts in the surface, and holes as big as basins. Edgar hated it, for he was old, and his springs were rusty. He bounced and shuddered and spluttered, but Charles was too busy rehearsing his opening speech to pay much attention to Edgar's bad temper. "I'm Charles Weatherby," he mouthed. "My Mother sent me to call on you — here is her letter — she's a bit of an invalid or she would have come herself." Then I hand her the letter and wait while she reads it. Then I say, "I do hope you can come" — I don't want her to come a bit, but I shall have to say it — that's what they call a white lie.

He steered Edgar between the crumbling gate-posts and drew up at the front door. The whole place looked frightfully neglected and overgrown; the paths were weedy, and the tall rhododendron bushes, with which the house was surrounded, seemed to have closed in upon it on all sides. Charles had not been here since his last leave, and he decided that the place had gone down hill a good deal; it was darker and damper and more dismal than he had thought. It was very quiet too, but in the distance he could hear the clang of hammers and the voices of men shouting, and he decided that they must be working at the new bridge. Dingleford Cottage was so mixed up in his mind with the Prestcotts that he could scarcely believe they were not here. He had seen them yesterday in their new abode, but their ghosts still lingered about the place where they had lived so long. Or perhaps it was not their ghosts — for living people can't have ghosts, can they? Perhaps Dingleford Cottage retained a sort of "Prestcott smell", just as a pigsty harbours the fragrance of its occupant long after that occupant has gone.

Charles rang the bell, and, almost immediately, the door was flung open by a small elderly woman with bright eyes, apple-cheeks and iron grey hair.

"Oh, 'ere you are at last!" she cried. "What a time you've took! Come upstairs quick and get to work."

"But I say —" Charles began, taken aback by this unexpected reception.

"Come along, will you."

"But look here . . . Look here, is Miss Fortune in? I've got a note —"

"Never mind all that now," cried the woman, seizing him by the sleeve and dragging him in. "There's been enough time wasted already — more than enough. The water 'as started drippin' through the ceiling. Such a 'ouse I never did see in all my life. 'Lizabethan my eye — it was built before Noah's flood, if you ask me. Everything wore out with age an' the very doorstep dented. Come on quick, do."

By this time Charles had ceased to expostulate — it was no use, for the woman was much too excited to listen to him. She had tight hold of his arm, and was dragging him up the stairs. Without physical violence, which he was too chivalrous to employ upon a member of the weaker sex, Charles had no option but to follow.

"Come on quick — don't dawdle — faster, faster," she cried, like the Red Queen, and so active was she despite her age, that Charles was quite breathless when they arrived at the top.

"'Ere we are!" said the little woman, "through this door — bend your 'ead, please; we don't want you brained till you've stopped the leak."

Charles bent his head obediently and entered a dim low-roofed attic with a small round window at one end. There was a queer splashing noise going on, and he was surprised to find that the floor was nearly ankle deep in water. He was aware that there was somebody else in the attic — Miss Fortune herself, he supposed — but it was obviously no time to greet her with his carefully rehearsed speech.

"What's the matter?" he asked bluntly.

"The tank . . . the cistern or whatever you call it. Oh please do something quickly."

He looked round and saw a large tank, balanced upon wooden props. It was obviously full of water, and more than full, for water was brimming over its iron sides and splashing onto the floor. The situation was really desperate and instant action was necessary. With a muttered curse, he strode across the floor, splashing the water in all directions, leapt onto the edge of the tank and plunged his arms into its depths. Fortunately he happened to know something of the working of cisterns, they had fascinated him in his extreme youth

— they and other intricacies of plumbing. Charles had been the sort of boy who loves to have workmen in the house and who follows them round with questions, pertinent and otherwise, until they are glad to depart. He remembered now that there ought to be a kind of ball, bobbing about on the top of the water — where was the blinking thing? He hung over the edge of the cistern and groped for it, with his legs in the air and the water splashing round. Where on earth was it? Ah, here it was, stuck down at the very bottom of the tank, with the arm, to which it was attached, firmly fixed. It was stuck so fast that at first he could not move it, so he jiggled it about and tugged again with all his might — and suddenly it was free. It rose to the top of the tank with a whoosh of water, the whole tank rocked, a huge wave rolled out and Charles took a half somersault backwards and landed on the floor with a splash.

"Blast!" said Charles firmly. There was a great deal more that wanted saying but he remembered in time that there were ladies present.

"Gracious, are you hurt?" exclaimed Miss Fortune.

"No-o," said Charles doubtfully. He scrambled up and stood there, dripping, with his hair plastered over his face in wet strands.

Meanwhile Miss Fortune was investigating the tank.

"You've stopped it!" she cried delightedly. "Look Nannie, he's stopped the water — it isn't running any more."

It was true. The water still slopped about the floor in waves made by the disturbance, but no more water was coming over the edge of the tank and the splashing sound had ceased.

"Well, I must say he's a quick worker for a plumber," Nannie announced. "I never saw no plumber tackle a job so strenuous in all my born days."

"But I'm not a plumber."

"There now, I knew 'e couldn't be!" cried Nannie, who seemed to have forgotten her obstinate conviction that he was.

"Do you mean that you aren't one of Mr. Saintsbury's men?" enquired Miss Fortune.

"No I'm —"

"Well, never mind who you are," she interrupted quickly. "You've done splendidly, and I'm most awfully grateful to you. Take him down to the kitchen, Nannie, and dry his clothes and give him something hot to drink."

"That's right," agreed the old woman briskly. "Tea with whisky in it is what you'll get. Come along quick now, and try and not drip on the carpet."

Charles said no more, but followed Nannie meekly.

He was cold and wet and all he wanted was a good fire and a hot drink. If these things were to be procured in the kitchen then the kitchen was the place for him. Later, when he was dry and warm he could make known his identity and deliver his message.

The kitchen was clean and cosy, and a gorgeous fire leapt and twinkled in the old fashioned grate. Nannie bustled about importantly. "There now," she said, "You take off your clo'es an' I'll soon get them dry . . . give me your trousers, that's right . . . I'll 'ave a cup o' tea

40

ready in two jiffs . . . lucky the kettle's on the boil . . . we don't want you catching a cold . . . let's 'ave your shoes . . . *Gracious!*"

"What's the matter?" Charles enquired.

She was looking at the shoes which he had handed to her, and now she raised her eyes to his face. "Oh, goodness, gracious!" she cried in consternation. "Goodness, gracious — you're a gentleman!"

It was the last straw to be recognised as a "gentleman" by his shoes. Charles, standing before the fire clad in Aertex underwear, began to laugh. He laughed as he hadn't laughed for years, until the tears streamed down his cheeks and he was doubled up with pain.

The old woman had to laugh too, for such gargantuan laughter is infectious, but she was very worried all the same. "But you are, aren't you?" she enquired.

The simple enquiry contributed to his mirth. "My shoes!" he explained between his painful spasms. "My shoes — ha ha ha!"

"I never looked at you, Sir, not proper," she assured him. "So worried I was, with the water coming through the ceiling. I was expectin' the plumber an' there you was, an' I thought it was 'im. Lor' 'ow awful! But I never looked at you for a moment . . . an' you plungin' into the water like that! Why, you might get your death!"

"Stop!" cried Charles. "Stop for Heaven's sake, Nannie. You'll give me my death with laughing. Why should I get my death plunging into the water any more than the wretched plumber?"

"A gentleman isn't accustomed to it," Nannie pointed out. "Oh dear, whatever shall I do! It's all my fault — not 'ers. Don't blame it on 'er, will you? She couldn't see you in the dark. It's all my fault."

"It's Edgar's fault," declared Charles weakly, his laughter had spent itself somewhat by this time.

"Edgar!" she exclaimed.

"Yes, but never mind, there's no harm done."

"'Arm!" cried Nannie. "I should just think there was 'arm done — I'll never get over it, never."

"Nonsense, Nannie!"

" 'Ow clever you are, too," she continued earnestly, "stoppin' that 'orrible leak. Oh dear me, whatever will Miss Jane say when she 'ears!"

"It's all right, I tell you."

"Such a dreadful thing to 'appen — and us just settlin' into a new place —"

"Will you stop it," cried Charles, seizing her by the arm and shaking her gently. "Will you stop it. I tell you THERE'S NO HARM DONE."

CHAPTER
SIX

Miss Fortune walked into the kitchen with a bottle of whisky in her hand. She had changed her wet clothes and was now spick and span, clad in a neat tweed skirt and a scarlet pullover. She was feeling very benevolent towards the plumber who had done her such yeoman service, but her benevolence vanished when she beheld the young man shaking Nannie by the arm, and she was rooted to the spot with horror. Charles, clad only in his underwear, was equally horrified at the sight of Miss Fortune. He was perfectly decent, of course — far more covered from view than if he had been arrayed in his bathing suit — but convention decrees that whereas bathing suits are proper garments in which to appear before a young unmarried lady, vests and pants are not.

"Stop that at once. Do you hear me!" cried Miss Fortune sharply.

Charles had already stopped shaking Nannie, and now he dropped her arm and stood there sheepishly, wishing that the kitchen floor would open and swallow him whole.

"It's all right!" cried Nannie, rushing to the defence of her assaulter. "'E wasn't doing nothing . . . Just being kind . . . telling me not to worry and all . . . but, oh dear, it's so awful what I've done . . . I'll never get over it, never . . . but it's all my fault, not yours . . . I've told 'im that."

"What's your fault, Nannie?"

"Oh gracious, I don't 'ardly know 'ow to tell you."

"Tell me *what?*" enquired Miss Fortune, naturally somewhat alarmed.

" 'E's a gentleman," Nannie declared dramatically. " 'E's a gentleman come to call . . . and just look at what we've done to 'im! Oh dear!" cried Nannie, wringing her hands in distress. "Oh dear . . . an' me thinking 'e was a plumber . . . and 'im so clever stoppin' the water . . . Oh dear!"

Miss Fortune took in the whole situation with remarkable rapidity — perhaps because she was used to Nannie's ways. She put the bottle on the table and smiled at Charles. "Oh! How *awful* of us!" she said.

It was the first time that Charles had really seen her, certainly the first time that he had seen her smile. She was exactly as Mrs. Prestcott had described her — fair curly hair, brown eyebrows, grey eyes, etc., but she was also incredibly more; incredibly different from the somewhat pert, pink and white Miss that he had visualised. Mrs. Prestcott had said nothing about her firm little chin, nor her adorably expressive mouth, nor the dimples that came and went when she smiled. Pretty creature, said Charles to himself, so bewitched that, for the moment, he forgot his deshabille, pretty pretty creature! It seemed to him that he knew exactly what she was like, inside as well as out, for when men admire beautiful women it is because they believe the beautiful casket to contain beautiful things. Charles was sure that the fair Miss Fortune was gold all through.

"It doesn't matter a bit," he babbled nervously. "I mean I'm frightfully glad I could help. I know a bit about cisterns and things, you see."

"Isn't that lucky!" she exclaimed, opening her eyes very wide.

He agreed that it was.

"It was frightfully kind of you," she added. "I really don't know *how* to thank you. Nannie and I were quite desperate."

"I don't wonder," declared Charles earnestly. "I don't wonder at all. Of course you were desperate — anybody would have been."

"And now we'll all have tea," she said firmly, "and you must have whisky, so that you won't get a chill. Hurry up, Nannie."

Nannie was chuckling with delight at the turn things had taken. The gentleman wasn't angry at all, in fact he was decidedly pleased to have been of service — such a nice gentleman he was too, such pleasant manners, and so well made. She took a glance at his legs as she bustled round the kitchen and decided that they were just right — neither too fat (which was horrible) nor too thin (which was worse). It wasn't often you saw legs like that. She had whipped out a snowy white cloth and spread it on the snowy white table — cups and saucers followed and all the impedimenta of a civilized meal. In a few moments the three of them were sitting at the table drinking tea and eating mixed biscuits out of a tin. Charles was perfectly happy now, for Miss

Fortune's disregard of her guest's unconventional attire was complete — and therefore reassuring — she behaved as if she were quite used to entertaining strange young gentlemen garbed in their underwear to tea in her kitchen at eleven o'clock in the morning.

The two of them explained to Charles exactly what had happened in a sort of duet. Miss Fortune began the tale by saying that they had arrived at the cottage last night and found the water "off" but, as they hadn't been able to find the "turning thing" they had left it and gone to bed "dead beat".

"Dead beat — and no wonder," added Nannie, nodding her head in profound agreement.

"We found the turning thing in the morning — it was in the coal cellar," continued Miss Fortune.

"And I turned it on," Nannie said.

The water had rushed in gaily, and gaily Nannie and Miss Fortune had started to "get things straight". Soon, however, the cistern had filled, and, not content with filling, had begun to overflow — it had been a frightful moment. Nannie had rushed out to the bridge and found a boy with a bicycle, and the boy had promised to fetch a plumber from Dingleford — the rest Charles knew.

"The waste pipe must be choked," said Charles thoughtfully. "I shall have to see to that."

"You'll do nothing of the kind," declared his hostess. "The plumber will be here any moment. You've done quite enough. It *was* lucky for us that you came when you did. Were you . . . did you . . ."

"I came to call, really," Charles told her, smiling at the thought of the formal speech which had never been delivered. "I've got a letter for you from my mother — it's in my pocket I expect."

The letter was not in his pocket, nor could it be found, but that was immaterial since Charles was conversant with its contents. He explained that it was an invitation to lunch, and that Edgar was waiting outside all ready to convey Miss Fortune to Sunnymead — "and I do hope you can come," he added earnestly, and with complete truthfulness.

"Yes . . . well . . . it's awfully kind, but what about Nannie?" Miss Fortune demurred. "There's such a lot to be done, you see —"

"Rubbish!" cried Nannie. "You go along with the young gentleman, Miss Jane. There's no 'urry about the work . . . I'll just see if 'is trousers is dry," and she bustled off into the scullery and vanished from sight.

"What an old dear!" Charles said in a whisper, and finding it so pleasant to whisper to Miss Fortune (pleasant to say "dear" to this delightful creature — even if he were not addressing it to herself) he continued in an even lower tone, which was quite unnecessary in view of the fact that Nannie was not there: "What a *darling!*"

"Oh she *is*," Miss Fortune agreed, nodding. "She was our nurse, and she's going to help me with the tea-shop. You know about the shop?"

"Yes, I know about it. I think it's a splendid idea," declared Charles. "I'll help too. I mean I'm quite good at — well — carpentry or anything like that . . . I mean

I could knock up a shelf for you or anything . . ." He stopped suddenly, for it dawned upon him that he was going too far and too fast. It would never do to frighten the dear little thing. She was so young, and so innocent.

Charles wished very fervently that she would go away while he put his trousers on (being drill, they had dried very quickly and Nannie, the good soul, had ironed a beautiful crease in them) but apparently she had no intention of going away so he had to make the best of it and dress as quickly and unobtrusively as possible. He covered up his nicely tanned, well-shaped legs with the hideous garments devised by civilised man and soon, shirted, trousered, jacketed, his face scrubbed clean, and his hair slicked into place with Nannie's comb, he was ready to escort Miss Fortune to his Mother's house.

Edgar behaved quite decently on the way home, but whether this was because he liked the look of Miss Fortune, or simply because he knew he was homeward bound it is difficult to say.

The luncheon party was a gay affair, for Emma had to hear the whole story of the morning's adventures, and the story lost nothing in the telling — such sagas never do. She listened to the recital of her son's prowess and skill as told by Miss Fortune with shining eyes. This is she, said Emma to herself, this is the very girl for Charles — so natural and friendly and amusing, and so adorable to look at — but I must be clever, she thought, I mustn't spoil it by trying to throw them together. I must watch and wait, and not interfere at all — there's plenty of time.

There was plenty of time for romance to materialise — if it was going to materialise at all — for Charles had eight months' leave ahead of him, but Emma rather overdid her cleverness. In fact, when Miss Fortune had departed, and they were discussing the events of the day, she responded to her son's panegyric of their guest so half-heartedly that he thought she had taken a dislike to the girl. He was worried, but not unduly, for he did not believe that anybody could fail to like Miss Fortune, if they saw enough of her. Emma was a reasonable woman, she would "come round" he felt sure.

CHAPTER
SEVEN

The next morning Charles appeared in Emma's room directly after breakfast, and she noted, with secret amusement, that he was wearing his best suit.

"Is there anything you would like me to do?" he enquired anxiously, "because, if not, I think I'll go down to Dingleford Cottage and have another look at that cistern. I've been thinking about it, and I feel we really ought to make sure that the ball is working properly — and the waste pipe, of course."

"What a bore for you!" exclaimed Mrs. Weatherby with a little frown.

"Yes, isn't it," agreed Charles, trying to look as if it were a bore and not succeeding, "but . . . well . . . what I feel is it's rather a pity for her to spend money getting Saintsbury."

"I should have let you be a plumber," declared Mrs. Weatherby with a sigh. "You wanted to when you were seven, and were quite angry with me for my lack of enthusiasm over the idea. Think of the money I should have saved on your education!"

"I know," said Charles, grinning, "the biggest mistake you ever made."

It was a temptation to Emma to comment on Charles' best suit, and to suggest, slyly, that the old drill slacks would be more suited to the work he had in hand, but she denied herself the pleasure and let him go in peace. He clattered off, whistling merrily and, Edgar proving strangely amenable, was soon well on his way.

It was a lovely sunny morning and it seemed to Charles that Dingleford had never looked so beautiful before. This was England to Charles — this little backwater where the old houses clustered round the village green, and the square towered church watched over them as a mother hen watches over her chicks — and Charles felt that England was well worth serving. He had lived so long in sun-baked lands that the brilliant green of his native land was almost incredible. It had rained a little in the early morning and the shower had freshened the grass and washed the white dust from the hedges and the trees. The trees were as proud as kings; they had given shade to Dingleford for two hundred years, and they looked good for another hundred at least. The houses which clustered round the green had mossy roofs, and diamond paned windows, and old oak beams, and little gardens bright with flowers; they were all different and were placed at different angles to the road: some facing it squarely, and others half turned away so that they presented an angle of wall to the beholder.

Charles knew the place well, of course, he had seen it a thousand times in every sort of weather, but today he saw it differently. It seemed more real, more beautiful,

51

more significant than it had ever seemed before. Charles wondered why this should be, but he had no time to solve the problem now, for there were other beauties than those of Dingleford (more warm and human) which he was impatient to see, so he put spur to Edgar and rattled off down the winding road which led to Miss Fortune's cottage.

Nannie received the visitor with open arms, but her news was not altogether acceptable. "Miss Jane's out," she said. "Now isn't that a pity? She's gone to do the shopping; she *will* be sorry to 'ave missed you, sir."

It was certainly a pity that Miss Fortune was out, but Charles was not to be got rid of so easily. "It's the cistern, really," he explained. "I think I'd better have a good look at it . . . Supposing it were to overflow again —" he added with consummate guile.

"Land Sakes — I 'ope not!" exclaimed Nanny.

"I'll just go up. Don't you bother," Charles told her, rummaging for some tools in the back of the car.

He went up through the house, and entered the attic where the cistern was. The window was open and the floor was almost dry; the cistern guggled and bubbled contentedly like a well fed infant. Charles found a chair to stand on and peeped into the tank, he was supplied with a torch today so that he could see what he was doing. He saw that the ball was working perfectly. He poked it down in the water and it bobbed up again as a properly conducted ball should do. Charles then examined the arm to which the ball was attached and discovered that it was rusty. This was fortunate, for it necessitated a descent to Edgar for an oil-can. Charles was much more like a real plumber today, for he did not hurry; he had realised that he must spin out his work until Miss Fortune should return — in fact Saintsbury himself could not have taken longer to fetch the oil-can and attend to the hinge. When that was done he had to test the ball again, and examine the waste pipe. He spent a long time playing about with the cistern, depressing the ball so that the tank filled and the water flowed away down the pipe — it was very pleasant, really, and brought back his childhood days. The attic was dark and quiet, but outside in the trees the birds were singing madly, and Nannie was bustling about down below in the kitchen clattering her pots and pans.

Miss Fortune was surprised but by no means displeased when she returned from her shopping expedition to find Edgar waiting in the drive. She recognised him at once, of course, for his lines were unorthodox to the modern eye.

"Hullo Edgar!" she said, patting his bonnet affectionately. "How are you feeling this morning? Is master here?"

"Yes," said Charles, putting his head out of the attic window and speaking in a hoarse croaking voice which he conceived to be the kind of voice which might emanate from Edgar, if Edgar, like Baalam's ass, could speak. "Yes, Miss Fortune, master's in the attic a-mending of the tank."

Miss Fortune was so startled at the unexpected reply that she dropped her parcels on the gravel. And then, recovering herself somewhat, she looked round and up and spied Charles' face grinning at her from the attic window.

"Oh Captain Weatherby, you wretch!" she cried, laughing heartily at the joke. "Oh you wretch — what a fright you gave me. Come down at once!"

The head disappeared from the window and Charles came clattering down the stairs.

"Did you really think it was Edgar?" he enquired.

"I believe I did — just for a moment," Miss Fortune admitted with twinkling eyes. "It was such a queer voice, so . . . so creaky, if you know what I mean. It sounded just the sort of voice that Edgar *would* have. And another thing, Edgar is so human — I expect you've noticed that — he's quite different from any other car that I've ever seen."

Edgar's owner agreed to this fervently.

Miss Fortune now showed Charles how she had arranged the house. The old drawing-room had been set aside for the tea-shop, it was empty at present, for the chairs and tables had not yet arrived; next door was the little parlour, and here were arranged Miss Fortune's household goods.

"It's cosy, isn't it?" Miss Fortune said, "but oh dear, I wish it were not so dark."

The two rooms faced towards the back of the house where the new road lay, but between the windows and the road there was a thick belt of tall rhododendron bushes. So although the rooms faced south, and the sun was shining brightly, it was almost as if one were under water, so dim they were, so greenly shaded.

54

Charles surveyed the bushes with a critical eye; they were very old, their stems were gnarled and twisted, and their huge green leaves were tattered with the passing of years. The bushes had always been there and Charles and Harold had played amongst them, crawling in and out of the home-made jungle like a couple of Sioux Braves. He remembered that there had been a clearing in the middle of the thicket where they had lighted a fire and roasted potatoes in an old tin tray. There were a thousand happy memories enshrined in that jungle, but Charles was a practical man.

"We'll cut the whole thing down," he said firmly.

"What!" cried Miss Fortune, horror-stricken at the boldness of the idea.

"Cut it down . . ." repeated Charles. "Root it up . . . clear it away! As a matter of fact you'll *have* to, or people won't see the house from the road; and if they don't see the house they won't stop for tea."

"I was going to have a board —" began Miss Fortune.

"No use," Charles declared.

"No use?"

"No. There must be a lawn here," he continued, sweeping away the whole tangled thicket with a wave of his hand, "a lawn with tea-tables and striped umbrellas — you know the kind of thing."

"It would be a frightful thing to do."

"You must do it, you simply must," he told her earnestly. Now that he had formulated the idea he was enchanted by it. He visualized himself cutting through the jungle with a saw, hacking down the bushes with an axe — and Miss Fortune watching him.

"Look at it!" wailed Miss Fortune. "Look at the thickness of the stems! Think of the roots! — and oh, whatever would Mrs. Prestcott say!"

"It's yours," he pointed out. "You've bought it. You can do what you jolly well please. I can do it easily — and I can get a man to help. As a matter of fact I know a man who would be thankful for the job — our gardener's brother. Then you'll get lots of sunshine in the house — the sun will stream in at the windows — think how lovely that will be."

"Y — yes," said Miss Fortune, wavering.

"I'll start now," declared Charles firmly. "I'll start on that bush nearest the parlour window — where's the saw?"

Nannie provided a saw, and they both watched while Charles prepared for the fray. He took off his coat, and his tie, and undid his collar, and he rolled up the sleeves of his pale blue shirt. "Now we're off!" he exclaimed. The saw bit into the old gnarled stem with a grating sound, and in a few minutes the first bush was down.

CHAPTER
EIGHT

One day, about a week later, Charles Weatherby and Jane Fortune might have been seen playing golf together on the Dingleford Golf Course. Their friendship had progressed rapidly and so had the clearing of the shrubbery at the cottage. Charles, aided and abetted by Mrs. Weatherby's gardener's brother, had sawed and chopped his way through the tangled jungle to the road. It remained, of course, to pull up the roots, plough the ground and prepare it for seeding — but Rome was not built in a day. Charles had enjoyed the work thoroughly. For one thing he loved sawing down trees (what man does not?) and for another thing he loved Jane Fortune.

Inside the cottage there was still much to be done. Emma Weatherby had been transported to the scene in Edgar, and had been consulted about curtains and china, and other important details. She had given much sensible advice and the loan of her sewing machine to run up the curtains, had partaken of a cup of tea and departed none the worse for the excitement.

But all work and no play is a bad policy, so Saturday had been set aside for golf, and Saturday, pleased at the honour, had dawned bright and beautiful as a new penny, to lure the workers from their toil.

"Your honour," Jane said as they reached the thirteenth tee and prepared to drive off. "You know, Charles, I feel as if I had been here for years. I feel as if I were going to be happy here."

"Of course you are," declared Charles beaming at her, "but then you would be happy anywhere."

"I haven't always been happy."

"Oh I say!" exclaimed Charles in consternation.

Jane laughed. "Everybody can't be happy all the time. It wouldn't be good for us."

"No, but you — I mean everybody ought to be nice to you —"

"It's your honour," said Jane firmly.

Charles sighed. He had been hoping to learn something more about Jane — the opening had seemed propitious — but she had shut the door in his face. He knew quite a lot about her by this time, for he had developed a diabolical guile in the art of eliciting information without appearing to ask leading questions, but the thing that he really wanted to know he could not find out. Convention forbade him to ask Jane whether she had ever been engaged, or even whether there was any man in whom she was especially interested. This worried Charles.

She was very young, of course, but so fatally attractive he could hardly believe that she had escaped from the fowler's snare.

"Go on, Charles, it's your honour," said Jane for the third time.

Charles played off. He hit the ball a terrific blow and it sailed away curling more and more to the right and ending up with a splash in the middle of the pond. It was almost inevitable that he should slice, for his thoughts were not on the game.

"Cricket!" exclaimed Charles fiercely.

Jane pricked up her ears — she was rather interested in the milder form of swears, and this was a new one on her.

"My old cricket cut," he elaborated. "The wretched thing always comes back if I'm not thinking."

"It is bad luck," said Jane, "and it was a new ball too — simply sickening!"

Her eyes were so large and dewy with sympathy that Charles could have kissed her there and then. In fact the impulse was almost irresistible.

"There's a boat, isn't there?" Jane continued. "Can't we go out and poke about? I know exactly where it is."

"It's no use —" began Charles — and then he stopped, for it struck him that to take Jane out in the boat would be rather pleasant. He could hand her in, and hand her out, and there would be far more opportunity to talk. "But what about our game?" he asked doubtfully.

"It's too hot for golf," Jane declared, "and you're much too good for me. You must give me a half next time."

Charles made no more objections and soon they were rowing out on the pond. It was very pleasant indeed, cool and quiet; the pond was surrounded by pine trees whose straight boles and dark green needles were reflected with faithful accuracy in the still water. Far away in the distance could be heard the voices of players on the course, and the click of a club striking a ball. They drifted about for a little looking for the ball and prodding up the muddy bottom with a net — a thing like a very strong butterfly net, screwed to a stout bamboo pole, which the club in a philanthropic mood had provided for the purpose. Jane landed a rusty tin and a child's shoe, but of the ball there was no sign.

Charles had known beforehand that he would never see it again so he bore the disappointment with equanimity. "I like water, don't you?" he said.

Jane nodded. "Fishing is fun when you catch lots of fish. We used to go to Scotland every year with my Father — we loved it. He's dead now. Mother died when we were very small."

"Who's we?" Charles enquired with interest.

"My sister and I. She's working in London. It's horrid to be parted for we've always been together — always — all our lives."

"Couldn't she come here and help with the tea-shop?"

"She is coming later — if it's a success — but you see we thought it was rather silly for her to give up her job until we found out whether the tea-shop would pay."

Charles nodded, he saw how right he had been to bring Jane out on the water, for he had collected quite a lot of information and might collect more. Meanwhile his thoughts flew wildly on and he settled the future of the sisters with great satisfaction to himself. When he and Jane were married and went to India the other girl would come to Dingleford and run the tea-shop with old Nannie — it would work out beautifully, he thought.

"Nannie and I are longing for her to come," Jane continued earnestly. "We're not very happy about her, all alone in London."

"No, of course not," Charles agreed. He waited a little, and then, as no more information was forthcoming, he said: "Go on, Jane."

"Go on where?"

"About — about yourself."

Jane laughed. "How insatiable you are — like the elephant's child — but there's nothing much to tell you. I've had rather a dull life, Charles — not like you. I'd like to see the world — all the interesting places that one reads about but you can't always do what you want, can you?"

"No, you can't," agreed Charles. He wanted to kiss Jane and it was impossible. How long must I wait, he wondered.

"Oh, but men are different," Jane declared. "Men can be soldiers or sailors and go all over the world."

"Women can be soldiers' wives."

"That isn't the same at all," said Jane promptly and vigorously. "Look Charles, somebody wants the boat."

Charles was suitably chastened. He looked over towards the boat-house and saw Erica Manley, and Mr. Ames standing on the landing-stage waving their arms. He shouted that he was coming and rowed back slowly and with considerable reluctance. Somehow or other he did not want to introduce Jane to Erica — nor to anybody else in Dingleford for that matter — but there was no way out of it.

"So this is the Fair Miss Fortune!" exclaimed Mr. Ames with deplorable facetiousness. "No misfortune for Dingleford I can see."

Jane smiled pleasantly — it was the sort of remark to which no possible answer could be found.

"D'you want the boat?" enquired Charles abruptly.

"If you've *quite* finished with it," Erica replied. "Mr. Ames seems to think it would be fun to do a little fishing in the mud."

"It was a new ball," said Mr. Ames unhappily, "but of course if you would rather not bother . . . it will be all the same a hundred years hence."

Erica laughed rudely. "That's all very well, but 'never say die' is another proverb," she declared. "Perhaps you'd forgotten that one. Come along, Mr. Ames — are you going to row, or shall I? Or shall we each take an oar? 'Many hands make light work', but 'Too many cooks spoil the broth' — how difficult it is to decide for the best!"

Mr. Ames laughed nervously. They got in and pushed off, leaving Charles and Jane standing on the landing stage together.

"She's very pretty," said Jane.

Charles laughed. "'Handsome is as handsome does,'" he declared, picking up the two bags of clubs.

Charles did not offer his guest any refreshment after their round. His lack of hospitality was due to the fact that he had caught sight of Colonel Staunton in the window of the lounge; why should he share his precious Jane with every Tom, Dick and Harry in the place? But Colonel Staunton was the sort of man who can scent a pretty woman a mile away, so, before Charles could get Edgar to start, there was a firm military crunching on the gravel path, and the gallant officer bore down upon them with a beaming smile. Charles had to introduce him of course, for colonels are colonels even if they are retired, and mere junior captains owe them a certain amount of deference.

"Come in," said Colonel Staunton, full of engaging hospitality. "Come in and have a drink — sherry or ginger beer — come along. You too, Weatherby, of course."

He would take no denial for he was accustomed to having his own way — being a colonel and a bachelor to boot — so Charles and Jane were hauled out of the car and carried off to the clubhouse. Here, just as Charles had foreseen, Jane was immediately surrounded by male members offering her light conversation and liquid refreshment. There was Colonel Staunton, of course, and Mr. Manley and Giles; there was Mr. Ruff and his brother-in-law (who was staying at the vicarage) and the two Wickhams. Charles was fed up. He sat down and ordered a whisky and soda — he had to pay for it himself too, for the Colonel was far too busy making himself pleasant to Miss Fortune to remember that he was supposed to be standing Charles Weatherby a drink.

Charles sipped his whisky and watched the scene with a jaundiced eye; what fools they were, standing round laughing and jabbering at Jane! Archie Wickham was exactly like a horse, with his long pale face and his sticking out teeth. Look at him throwing back his head and neighing! As for Mr. Ruff, thought Charles, he ought to know better than to make an exhibition of himself in the clubhouse lounge — a clergyman, thoroughly married, with three children to his credit (though precious little credit could be given for those egregious Ruff kids!) The brother-in-law annoyed Charles even more, because he was really rather a decent looking chap and Jane seemed to be talking to him a lot.

"You're coming to the dance, of course," said Giles Manley.

"As my guest," declared Colonel Staunton. "I insist —"

"A dance — how lovely!" cried Jane. "Where and when?"

"It's the Golf Club Dance. We have it here annually," Archie Wickham replied.

"I'll come and fetch you in my car," said Giles Manley.

"No, no, my dear feller. That will be my pleasure," Colonel Staunton declared. "Miss Fortune is coming as my guest."

"How nice of you all!" Miss Fortune said, smiling at them in her charming way.

The wretched Charles was furious to think that he had not already invited Jane to the dance. He had intended to take her, of course, but had forgotten to mention it, and now she was going with Colonel

Staunton — Colonel Staunton if you please! Oh hell, muttered Charles in disgust. He was even — somewhat unreasonably — annoyed with the fair Miss Fortune herself. She might have *known* I was taking her, he thought, gnawing his thumb in his vexation.

At last the passage of time put an end to his misery. Miss Fortune withdrew herself from her circle of admirers and Charles was permitted to drive her home. If she were conscious of his gloom she did not show it, but talked quite pleasantly and admitted that she was very fond of dancing. "Are you going to the dance?" she enquired.

"Er — no," replied Charles. He regretted this piece of folly as soon as it was uttered.

"What a pity!" said Jane casually.

CHAPTER
NINE

A gentle shower of cards now began to fall at Dingleford Cottage, for the female population of Dingleford had been bullied or cajoled by its male relatives into calling upon Miss Fortune. Miss Fortune was at home when Miss Ames came, and liked her. They talked golf and gardens. She was out when Mrs. Manley — most reluctantly — left cards.

Mrs. Prestcott was early on the field. She sallied forth to call upon the new owner of her old home with the faithful Harold driving the car. It seemed to both of them that the cottage had shrunk considerably since they had left it, and that the trees and bushes had crept nearer to the front door.

"We were right to move," declared Mrs. Prestcott as she slid from her seat and rang the bell.

Harold agreed.

They rang the bell for some time without getting any reply and eventually concluded that it must be out of order — they knew its little ways only too well. Mrs. Prestcott was of a tenacious disposition, however, so instead of leaving her card on the mat (Harold's suggestion) she decided to walk round the house and find Miss Fortune herself. They walked round, Mrs.

Prestcott leading the way with her graceful gliding gait, Harold trotting along behind, somewhat worried at the idea of trespassing upon the privacy of Miss Fortune.

They had found the front of the house unchanged since their tenancy, but it was not so with the back. Here the alterations were so startling that the Prestcotts were frozen in their tracks. It was a scene of desolation that met their eyes, a scene of destruction and vandalism.

"Oh heavens!" exclaimed Mrs. Prestcott in dismay.

"Oh, how d'you do!" Miss Fortune said, appearing from behind a huge pile of cut rhododendrons and offering her hand. "How nice of you to call, Mrs. Prestcott! I'm afraid you must think it is awful of me to cut down these lovely shrubs of yours, but the truth is I felt so shut in. You see," she continued, babbling nervously, "you see, the poor little cottage has got to turn back to front because the back of it faces the road and has got to be the front."

"Yes," said Mrs. Prestcott, in a dazed way.

"On the other hand —" said Charles, appearing from behind the bushes, clad in an open necked shirt and khaki shorts, and carrying an enormous saw, "on the other hand I've been pointing out to J — Miss Fortune that the back of the cottage is every bit as pretty as the front, so it really ought to be grateful to us for revealing its beauties to the world."

"Doesn't he talk nonsense?" enquired Miss Fortune sweetly. "Of course you think it's frightful — I should hate it if I were you. I saw at once that I must cut down the bushes before they flowered or I should never have the heart to do it at all."

"But why do it at all?" asked Mrs. Prestcott with asperity.

"She must have sunshine," Charles explained. "*You* can understand that, of course, being a sun-worshipper yourself."

"Of course it looks dreadful *now*," Miss Fortune apologised, "but once the rubbish has been carted away —"

"She's going to have a lawn," Charles put in, waving his hands in an explanatory manner, "a lovely green lawn, stretching down to the road, with little tea tables, and yellow umbrellas."

Mrs. Prestcott shuddered, "Come Harold," she said firmly. "We must not interrupt the work."

"Oh, *do* stay and have tea — it will be ready in a minute," cried Miss Fortune hospitably.

"No," said the lady. "No, I think not. It has been a shock . . . some other day perhaps." And despite all entreaties she took her departure then and there.

Harold followed her miserably. Miss Fortune was the prettiest girl he had ever seen, and he would have liked to see more of her, but he knew that his Mother was smouldering with rage and might flare up at any moment, so although he wanted to stay he was even more anxious to be gone before any untoward incident occurred. Harold knew his Mother so well that he understood exactly why she was angry. It was not because she thought that Miss Fortune had erred in cutting down the shrubbery, but because it was really a great improvement. The bushes were a common variety of rhododendrons, and flowered sparingly owing to age and overcrowding, so that they were no loss, and by sweeping them away Miss Fortune had opened up the view and allowed the sun into the house. For years the Prestcotts had dwelt in damp twilight mitigated only by oil lamps, and the idea that anything else was possible had never once crossed their minds. What fools we were, thought Harold to himself, no wonder poor Mother is annoyed!

Some days later, Charles, arriving prepared for an afternoon's work amongst the rhododendrons, found Miss Fortune dressed in her best, sallying forth to return calls. He tried to turn her from her grisly purpose without effect, and at last in sheer desperation offered to accompany her.

"No Charles," said Jane firmly, "It wouldn't do at all. It's frightfully sweet of you of course — positively heroic — but it wouldn't do," and she tripped away, looking exceedingly nice, and left Charles to his own devices.

There was a path through the woods to the Manleys' house which was her first port of call, and, as the weather had been fine and dry, it was a pleasant walk. The house was very large — a great grim barrack of a place — but the grounds in which it stood were really lovely. Jane admired the flowers and looked at the smooth green lawns with wistful envy — her own smooth green lawn, on the subject of which Charles was so optimistic, and lyrical, seemed more than ever a distant and impossible dream.

Miss Fortune was considerably annoyed when it was disclosed to her by the portly butler, that Mrs. Manley was at home, for she had called early in the afternoon actuated by the unworthy hope that Mrs. Manley would be invisible (elderly ladies often take a siesta after lunch). It was even more unfortunate that the entire Manley family was congregated in the drawing-room when Jane arrived, for the Manleys en masse were somewhat overpowering. The four of them were always at loggerheads, and were openly rude to each other both in private and in the presence of strangers, and today, when the unfortunate Miss Fortune was announced, they were in the very middle of a first class row. She was aware of electricity in the atmosphere the moment she crossed the threshold, and her heart sank into her neat little box calf shoes. Father Manley was standing on the hearth rug, crimson in the face, his small eyes bloodshot like those of a boar at bay. Mother Manley was half buried in a large chair, hovering on the brink of tears, while Giles and Erica sprawled upon the sofa, sullen and defiant as a pair of tiger cubs.

It really was rather like entering a wild beasts' cage and Miss Fortune wished that she had stayed at home or, alternatively, had brought Charles to take care of her.

"Ahem! Pleasant weather we are having!" said Mr. Manley, almost choking in the effort to swallow a cutting sentence which he was about to deliver before Miss Fortune appeared.

"Yes, isn't it!" agreed Jane brightly, as she shook hands all round and took a chair.

"I find the temperature pleasant," suggested Mr. Manley.

"And the country is looking beautiful," declared his guest.

She was aware, the moment she had said it, that somehow or other she had blundered. The remark seemed perfectly harmless but the tension in the room increased.

"I agree with you, Miss Fortune," declared Mr. Manley, "the country *is* looking beautiful, but some people are blind to the beauties of nature."

"Not blind to them, sick of them," said Erica with vigour.

"Now Erica!" whimpered Mrs. Manley nervously.

Giles sat up and glared. "There are some people," he declared, "who would like to see the beauties of other countries besides their own, and other people who — like cows — are content to chew the cud in one field for ever."

"Are you calling me a cow?" enquired his father furiously.

"Dear me, no," replied Giles, raising his eyebrows in amazement. "I was merely making a general statement producing a little pleasant conversation for our guest."

"He's a bull," put in Erica, *sotto voce*.

"What did you say, Erica?" cried Mr. Manley, turning to gore her with his horns.

Mrs. Manley plunged into the conversation. "Are you — have you travelled much?" she enquired with a forced smile.

Jane admitted that she had been in France last year, and on being pressed for details gave a reluctant account of her trip. She realised that the subject was an unfortunate one but she could scarcely refuse to answer her hostess's questions, and her heart was fluttering so uncomfortably in her breast that she could think of no possible way of changing the subject.

"You *see*," said Erica at last, when the halting odyssey had come to an end. "Everybody has been abroad except us."

"I see no such thing," replied Mr. Manley promptly. "I see that Miss Fortune has been abroad, but she does not seem very enthusiastic about her travels. I also see that you, Erica, are singularly ill-grounded in the rudiments of English Grammar."

"I don't speak like a pedantic professor —" Erica began.

"Nor even like a well-educated woman," agreed Mr. Manley acidly. "In fact it seems that the money spent upon your education has been thrown away. I suggest that you study the grammar of your own tongue before setting out to a foreign land."

"Are you fond of dancing, Miss Fortune?" enquired Giles in a loud voice which almost — but not quite — drowned Erica's spirited reply to the effect that you did not speak your own language in a foreign land.

"Yes, I like dancing," Miss Fortune replied. She was too frightened of saying something controversial to elaborate her statement in any way, but apparently this subject was also a sore one with the Manleys.

"So do we," declared Giles, looking at his father in a significant manner.

"Dancing!" exclaimed that worthy, rising gamely to the bait. "You call it dancing! Perambulating round the room, clasping each other round the neck is not my idea of dancing. Why you should want to hie off to London to overheated restaurants to take part in such an orgy is more than I can see. Real dancing is a vanished art —"

"He means Folk Dancing — maypoles and things," gibbered Mrs. Manley. "My husband is a great authority upon old English customs."

"How interesting!" Miss Fortune exclaimed.

"This comfortable house —" Mr. Manley was saying, apropos of nothing in particular, "every luxury you can want — and all you think of is getting away."

"I hate the house," declared Erica amiably. "It's a great ugly barrack of a place — nobody could be happy here."

"I am perfectly happy," its owner pointed out.

"But you aren't sensitive to psychic atmosphere," said Giles with a wolfish smile.

"Psychic fiddlesticks!" Mr. Manley exclaimed. "What's the matter with the house? It's dry and comfortable —"

"There's a horrid feeling about it," Erica said.

Jane agreed with her — but not vocally of course — the house felt nasty, but whether this was due to its occupants or because there really was evil in its fabric she could not tell.

"You may not believe it of course," declared Giles, "but the psychic atmosphere of old houses is a scientific fact —"

Jane rose to her feet. The conventional ten minutes was barely over — in fact she saw by the clock on the mantelpiece that it was exactly nine and a quarter minutes since she had entered the room — but she could endure no more. If the Manleys wished to discuss psychic atmosphere they had better do it in private. Her presence did not seem to cramp their style very much, but still —

"So sorry you must go," said Mrs. Manley with obvious relief. "You must come again soon — to tea."

Jane murmured polite thanks, but declared that she was busy settling in, and, when asked to fix a distant date, added mendaciously that she was going away.

"Stick to that," Erica advised, "and have plenty more excuses up your sleeve. Mother never takes a hint, you know. She simply can't believe that everybody isn't pining to come and have tea with her. You'll get weak tea flavoured with straw, and rock buns with little black stones in them, and perhaps, if cook happens to be in a good temper," continued Erica wildly, "you'll be offered cold hot-buttered-toast stuck down to a silver dish with its own grease."

There was silence for a moment, blank horrified silence, and then Mrs. Manley gave a forced laugh. "Erica is so witty!" she exclaimed.

Jane shook hands all round and fled with such speed that the portly butler summoned to show her out had to make a sprint down the whole length of the hall to beat her to the door.

After this experience her call upon Miss Ames was comparatively uneventful. Brother and sister were both in, and welcomed their guest cordially. Their somewhat pedantic, old-fashioned courtesy to her, and to each other, made a very pleasant impression upon Jane, very pleasant indeed, and the thought crossed her mind that she had never met such a delightful pair in all her life.

Mrs. Wickham and Mrs. Prestcott were both out, and that finished the afternoon's work. Jane returned to Dingleford Cottage in time for tea hoping that Charles would be still there to share her meal and to listen to all her adventures. But Charles had got tired of sawing up bushes unseen and unadmired, and had gone to pay his long delayed call upon Widgett at the "Cat and Fiddle".

PART TWO

CHAPTER
TEN

It was a Tuesday afternoon and Dingleford village was drowsing in the sunshine. A few children were playing somewhat languidly upon the green, and a few women were leaning over their garden gates watching the children and carrying on desultory conversations with their neighbours. There was only one shop in Dingleford, but what a shop! It sold everything that the heart of man — or woman — could desire, and Mrs. Trail the owner of this rural emporium was also the Postmistress. She had lived in Dingleford all her life, and in all that time she had only been twice to London. The shop, which had been in her family for several generations, was really the old Ford House and had been converted gradually and without any major alterations into its present state. The whole of the ground floor, with the exception of a tiny parlour at the back, had been usurped by the growth of stock, and, by knocking down the partitioning walls, had been made into one large room where Mrs. Trail's business was conducted. Fortunately the old house possessed bow windows fronting the green, and Mrs. Trail's husband — a joiner by trade — had fitted up neat shelves to these windows so that more goods could be displayed.

The counter had been instituted by Mrs. Trail's grandfather; it was made of the best oak obtainable — any London cabinet maker's mouth would have watered if he had laid eyes upon it.

On this particular afternoon Mrs. Trail was dozing in the back-parlour when the tinkle of a bell announced that a customer had arrived.

"Drat!" said Mrs. Trail, stirring in her chair. "Drat — it's them kids for bull's eyes — Drat!" She rose slowly to her feet and waddled into the shop prepared to be short and sharp with her untimely visitor. Her annoyance vanished like magic however when she saw who it was that had disturbed her rest, and the grim expression which sat so strangely upon her round good-natured face was replaced by a beaming smile.

"Captain Weatherby!" she exclaimed. "Well there now — 'ow are you, sir? Mr. Widgett was sayin' you was home, an' I ses to Mr. Widgett 'Time flies' I ses, 'it ain't so very long ago but what 'e was coming to me for bull's eyes' I ses an' now it's you for beer."

"But I still like bull's eyes," Charles declared laughing. "Here I am, you see —"

"Well I never! D'you mean to tell me you want bull's eyes?"

"Of course I do. A quarter of your best."

"We've got the tobacco licence now," Mrs. Trail told him, pausing as she reached for the big glass bottle on the shelf. "Wouldn't you rather have a nice packet of Yellow Tigers, Capting? They'd be more in your line."

Charles hid a shudder. "Bull's eyes for me," he said firmly.

Mrs. Trail took her time about the transaction but her customer did not mind; he leant upon the counter and watched her weighing out his purchase in her slow unhurried way. Charles liked the shop, he had always been intrigued by the strange conglomeration of goods which were to be seen on the shelves, or hanging from hooks in the ceiling. The smell was interesting too; it was such a peculiar mixture. He sniffed and wondered: coffee, of course and onions and blacking and ham — these were easy to guess — but there was also a queer rubbery sort of odour which puzzled him a good deal until he spied a string of galoshes which dangled from the roof like a swarm of gigantic bees.

His purchase completed Charles stayed on for a little chat, for Mrs. Trail was one of his oldest friends and he was interested in people and their doings. He wondered suddenly what she thought about, apart from the shop — had she any relations? Had she any private life at all? She must have, of course, but it was exceedingly difficult to believe.

"How are things doing?" Charles enquired.

"Moderate, sir, thanking you," she replied politely. "It's difficult nowadays, with cars an' buses an' what not. People get into 'orbury so easy, you see, an' they likes buyin' their things in 'orbury — they thinks it's cheaper. Well, p'raps it is a bit, reely, but not if they adds on the bus fare — which they don't. An' then what 'appens if they wants somethin' in a 'urry?"

"They come to you of course."

She nodded. "They comes to me. An', if I 'ain't got it in stock, it's 'Oh Mrs. Trail, but you always used to 'ave spades' (or teaspoons or babies' shoes, or whatever it may be) an' what 'appens then?" demanded Mrs. Trail dramatically.

"Then *you* say," replied Charles, warming up to the game, "*you* say 'Yes, and you always used to buy spades and teaspoons and babies' shoes here, and now you go to Horbury.'"

"Well, you are a one, I must say," exclaimed Mrs. Trail laughing heartily. "'Owever did you know that?"

"Galoshes now," continued Charles, pointing to the string of rubber footwear which had intrigued him so much. "Have you a ready sale for galoshes?"

"Not exactly *ready*," replied Mrs. Trail gravely, "but there's times when I sells them pretty free. A sudden 'eavy plump after a dryish spell an' there'll be one or two customers askin' for galoshes."

"It's very dry just now —"

"Yes, it's dry; but I sold a pair yesterday jes' the same — you do get sales sometimes that you ain't expectin' — it was that new lady, Miss Fortune, she was in for a bit of 'am, an' she ses: 'Oh, I see you 'ave galoshes!' she ses. I fitted 'er out with a nice pair — size twos — which I 'ain't never thought I would get rid of, them bein' so small. A tiny foot she's got!"

"Yes — yes, hasn't she?"

"A tiny foot for 'er size, an' well-shaped too," agreed Mrs. Trail nodding seriously. "Why, gracious me! Talk of angels . . . if this 'ain't Miss Fortune 'erself!"

Charles swung round as the shop door opened, and beheld the graceful form and the sweet face that he had grown to know so well. He started forward with a glad cry of surprise. "Hullo, where are you off to?" he enquired.

The question was not altogether a rhetorical one, for Miss Fortune certainly looked as if she were "off to" somewhere very special. She was dressed in a smart navy-blue costume, and a navy-blue hat with a crimson wing was perched upon her curls. Charles had never seen this outfit before, and he had never seen Miss Fortune looking so smart. She was always neatly clad, of course, but today she was more than neat — in fact, there was no shadow of doubt but that Miss Fortune was dressed to kill.

She did not reply to Charles' cheerful greeting, but drew back a little and gazed at him somewhat blankly. It was dark in the shop compared to the bright glare of the village street, so perhaps she could not see.

"Hullo!" he said again. "Can't you see me in the dark?" and he laughed a trifle nervously for the blank gaze had alarmed him.

"Oh, it's you!" she exclaimed. "No, I couldn't see you."

"Where are you going?"

"Er — I'm just going — home."

He was longing to ask where she had been, togged up in all her finery, but somehow or other he couldn't do it. Her manner was so odd, she seemed to have withdrawn into herself — she seemed to be shut in behind a high wall. What on earth was the matter? Had he offended her in some way?

"I'm off up to town on Thursday," he continued, nervously. "It's a frightful nuisance because of the work, but Robertson knows what to do — he can get on with that root, can't he?"

"Yes," agreed Miss Fortune, showing a singular lack of interest in the news.

"I'm awfully sorry about it, but I must go — it's some business for Mother, you see."

Miss Fortune said she saw.

"Was the galoshes all right?" enquired Mrs. Trail.

"Oh yes — the galoshes — yes, splendid," declared Miss Fortune, turning away from Charles, and smiling prettily at the old woman. "Galoshes are so useful, aren't they?"

"Are they for working in the shrubbery?" asked Charles. It was rather a foolish question, because they could not be for anything else, but Charles wanted to say something and he could find nothing else to say.

"Yes, for working in the shrubbery," agreed Miss Fortune.

She made her purchase — a card of darning silk — and waited in silence while it was parcelled and her change counted out, not looking at Charles, but tapping her foot impatiently — or was it nervously — on the floor.

Charles was frightfully worried by her strange behaviour but he could say nothing in front of Mrs. Trail. He decided to wait until Jane left the shop and then follow her and ask what he had done to offend her. He waited, watching Mrs. Trail's clumsy fingers fumbling with the string. When the parcel was ready Miss Fortune took it and fled, and Charles, full of eagerness to explain and be forgiven for whatever he had done, grabbed his bull's eyes and followed her — but only as far as the door. Outside in the road there was a small blue sports car, and in the car a MAN. He was a pale young man with a high forehead and shiny black hair, the sort of hair that Charles had always detested — patent leather hair. Miss Fortune slid into the seat beside him and banged the door, and immediately the car sped off like an arrow and vanished in a cloud of dust.

The small blue sports car, with the shiny haired man at the wheel, buzzed gaily along the road to Dingleford Cottage.

Its occupants talked in the desultory manner of old friends —

"What ages you were in that shop!" said Shiny Hair casually.

"I know, couldn't help it."

"What a frightful road! I say you *will* let me know if you're coming up to town."

"I will . . . but I shan't be coming. You know why."

"I wish you would be sensible about it," the young man declared.

"I *am* sensible," she replied firmly. "Really, Jack, there's no good talking about it any more. The whole thing's settled."

When at last, almost shaken to pieces, they reached the cottage, and the car stopped outside the front door, Miss Fortune stepped out and shook herself. "Well, goodbye Jack," she said. "It was frightfully good of you to bring me."

The young man looked a little taken aback — perhaps he had hoped for an invitation to enter and partake — but he accepted his dismissal quite meekly. "So long!" he observed.

"You won't breathe a word?"

"I'll be silent as the grave. You know you can trust me, old thing."

"I know I can — and I'll write — perhaps," said Miss Fortune with a sweet smile. She had lifted a small suitcase out of the car and she stood with it in her hand while the little car backed and manoeuvred and shot out at the gate, then she turned with a swift graceful movement and ran into the house.

And now a very strange phenomenon might have been seen, if anyone had been there to see it — a phenomenon so curious, so incredible that "anybody" must have believed himself to be suffering from some frightful derangement of the optic nerve; for, coming down the steep wooden stair, with her hand on the carved wooden bannister was Miss Fortune . . . and coming in at the front door, stooping a little and peering into the gloomy hall was Miss Fortune. They saw each other at the same moment, and emitted the same ecstatic cry: "Darling, how lovely!" and a second later were enfolded in each other's arms.

CHAPTER
ELEVEN

Arms entwined the two Miss Fortunes drifted into the sunny little parlour where tea was laid. They sat down on the sofa, chattering like a pair of lovebirds and drank their tea from the same cup — for the second Miss Fortune's arrival was completely unexpected and there was only one cup on the tray.

The two Miss Fortunes were twins, of course, and identical twins at that. In every smallest detail the ravishing charms of our old friend, Miss Jane Fortune were duplicated in the face and figure of Miss Joan. They were not only as alike as two peas, for two peas out of the same pod may differ slightly in size and shape, they were as alike as two silver sixpences minted on the same day from the very same die and found by the good child in its Christmas stocking. So much for their outward shape; their inward shape and expression, and the aura of their personalities were less alike. Jane was the elder by half an hour and, as such more dependable than Joan, she was quieter and stronger in character, less vivacious, more assured. Joan had always been the mischievous one, the gay spark, bubbling over with laughter and the joy of life. The difference was very slight, and now, when both were excited by the pleasure of seeing each other, there was scarcely a pin to choose between their vivacity and verve.

"My dear!" cried Jane. "I've been pining for you . . . four solid weeks since I've seen you . . ."

"My darling, what adventures I've had! I must tell you the whole thing . . ." cried Joan.

The sound of their voices brought Nannie from the kitchen where she was stringing beans, and she was immensely delighted to find that her "baby" had arrived. There were more huggings and kissings and more bubbling laughter, but at last the newcomer was persuaded to sit down quietly like a reasonable being and explain her presence at Dingleford.

"I'm sacked," she declared. "Well, really, I suppose I've sacked myself, because I just got into Jack's car and *came*. I couldn't bear it any longer — not one moment."

The hat shop, in which Miss Joan Fortune had obtained a job, belonged to a Frenchman, Monsieur Delaine. He was not a nice Frenchman (as Joan was careful to explain), not small and neat and courteous, as Frenchmen ought to be, but large and rude and bullying, as they most certainly ought not.

"Was he rude to you?" asked Jane, her eyes flashing fire at the mere thought of it.

"No," said Joan. "No, not rude a bit. I only wish he *had* been rude."

Nannie and Jane looked at each other in dismay — it was even worse than they had feared.

"He's mad," declared Joan, shaking her golden head so that her curls bobbed up and down like glinting sunshine. "He's stark staring mad. I was so frightened of him that I ran away."

"But surely —" Jane began.

"No, it was no *good*. I told him I didn't like him a bit, and he didn't believe me. So then I said I would go away, and he would never see me again if he didn't behave, and he said —" declared Joan, gazing at them with large eyes, "— he said he would follow me and find me wherever I went because he couldn't live without me."

"Goodness!" exclaimed Jane and Nannie with one accord.

"So then I ran away," said Joan frankly. "I was frightened, you see. Jack brought me here in his car . . . and here I am."

"And here you'll stay," said Jane, comfortingly. "It's lovely having you, just *lovely*."

"Nobody need know that I'm here, need they? We won't tell anybody —"

"Now just you listen to me," Nannie broke in. "There's no need to talk of nobody knowing you're 'ere. The man isn't going to follow you — and even if 'e does, what's the 'arm? I'll see to 'im," she added boldly.

"You don't understand a *bit*," wailed Joan. "He's mad, I tell you, and as strong as ten horses."

A long talk followed. Nannie and Jane tried to persuade her that she was safe at Dingleford Cottage, and Joan declared, almost hysterically, that she was safe nowhere from the unwelcome attentions of Monsieur Delaine.

"Well 'ow are we to 'ide you?" Nannie demanded at last, her patience almost exhausted with the struggle. "'Ow are we to 'ide you 'ere? Why, everybody in Dingleford knows what everybody else is doin'."

"They won't know I'm here if they don't see me," said Joan firmly.

The two girls were so delighted to see each other again and had so much to say that they talked solidly all the evening. They talked of everything that had happened since last they met, and Joan suddenly remembered that she had never said a word about the encounter with the brown-faced man in the Dingleford shop.

She repaired her omission at once, giving full details.

"It was Charles," said Jane, recognising him immediately. "Oh darling, were you nasty to him?"

"No — o," replied Joan doubtfully. "I didn't exactly fall upon his neck, of course. It was rather difficult to know how well I knew him — never having seen him before."

Jane realised the truth of this. "Poor Charles!" she sighed. "He really has been such a help, cutting down trees and things."

"Heavens, should I have known him as well as that!" cried Joan in mock dismay.

At ten o'clock Nannie appeared to say that it was time for bed and they were both amazed to find that it was so late.

It never occurred to them to dispute Nannie's right to interfere, for the habit of obedience to her word was deeply ingrained, and, although they were now "grown-up" and Nannie received her wages from Jane every month in the usual manner of paid dependants, she still ruled them in all the minor details of life with an iron hand.

"Oh Nannie, need we?" cried Joan, as if she were a child of nine instead of a grown woman of nineteen years.

"Yes, you must," declared Nannie firmly. "Go along now — both of you," and then, relenting a little she added, "You can put on your dressing-gowns and come down and 'ave your 'ot milk in the Parlour. Go along now, quick do."

They went along obediently, and returned garbed in pyjamas and pale blue silk dressing-gowns of exactly the same pattern, for it was a favourite custom of theirs to have all their clothes the same. And now that they were dressed alike, and Joan had cast off her London garments, the likeness between them was even more remarkable. Nannie brought in the hot milk and smiled at them benignantly — she always knew them apart, though how she accomplished this apparently impossible feat she never revealed. "Nannie knows us by our smell," Joan had once declared to a somewhat inquisitive old lady who had pestered her with questions on the subject, and this was perhaps the best attempt to explain the inexplicable.

The little supper in the parlour was a great success, it was so pleasant, in fact, that a precedent was established, and Nannie lived to regret her folly in making the suggestion.

★　★　★

The morning after Joan's arrival at Dingleford was bright and sunny, and there was sunshine inside the cottage as well as out. The necessary housework was soon done and Jane set off to the village with her shopping bag over her arm while Joan repaired to the parlour with a roll of gaily coloured cretonne to "run up" some curtains on Mrs. Weatherby's sewing machine. She was very happy today, for she felt at home and safe, lapped about with Jane's love and Nannie's familiar authority. Her short spell of "being on her own in London" to which she had looked forward with great excitement, had proved a complete failure from Joan's point of view. Homesick, lonely and considerably frightened, pining for her twin every hour of the day, she had been in no mood to go about with Jack and enjoy herself as she had planned.

A few bees buzzed in and out of the open window, and the sewing machine buzzed too. In the kitchen Nannie clattered her pans and sang — slightly out of tune as ever. It was all very peaceful and secure.

Joan had finished one curtain and was starting on the second when a slight noise caused her to raise her head, and she saw a man standing at the window, looking in. Her first instinct was flight (for, although the man was a complete stranger and in no way resembled her pursuer, the fact that she was in hiding was clearly in her mind) but before she had time to rise from her chair, she perceived that her safest course was to remain where she was. The man would think she was Jane . . . if he knew Jane . . . if he didn't know Jane he would think so all the more. Her reasoning, if slightly muddled, proved sound.

"I say! I rang the bell, but it didn't ring," said her visitor, somewhat nervously.

"Oh, I am sorry!" Joan exclaimed.

"It's always going wrong," he continued. "The wires get caught, you know — I could put it right for you in a moment."

"How kind of you!"

She was completely at a loss. Did Jane know the man or not? Could he possibly be some kind of plumber, cadging for a job? . . . but no, he was obviously a man of her own class. By this time he had climbed in through the window and was standing before her, smiling at her with eyes which were as brown and softly appealing as a spaniel's pup's. He was dressed (she noticed) in a suit of Harris Tweed plus fours with hairy stockings and nailed shoes. Joan liked the look of him, she liked his brown wavy hair, and she liked his doggy eyes. She liked also the faint air of shyness and indecision that hung about him, for she was fed up with he-men at the moment.

"How nice of you to call!" she said, smiling at him in a friendly way.

"Oh it's nothing — I mean I was passing," he stammered, and then, appearing suddenly to change his mind, he drew himself up and declared gruffly, "No, that's a lie. I wasn't passing at all, I came to see you . . . I wanted to."

"That's even nicer of you," said Joan. She was much amused to think of the havoc wrought upon the youth of Dingleford in one short month by the Fortune charms. There was "Charles" for instance whom she had already seen — Charles Somebody, with a brown face and white teeth who came and sawed down trees for Jane's sweet sake — and now there was this man offering to mend the bell. He was quite a different type, of course, somewhat shy, but possessing a kind of desperate boldness which the shy sometimes exhibit at unexpected moments. Yes, this man certainly had his points — the flavour of his unexpectedness was undeniably attractive.

"Sit down, won't you!" Joan invited, sweeping the roll of cretonne off a chair.

The man sat down. "It's a great improvement," he said, pointing somewhat vaguely to the window. "I wanted to tell you that . . . that I think it is. Of course we were used to them, so we never thought about it . . . but they made the place damp . . ." he stopped and looked at her beseechingly.

"Yes, of course," Joan soothed, wondering what on earth he was talking about.

"It *was* dark," he continued reminiscently. "Of course Mother used to say it was restful . . . but she can't say that now of course." He laughed and Joan laughed too, wishing that she had some idea what the joke was.

"Rather amusing, really," declared her visitor, who was beginning to lose his nervousness. "Rather amusing when you think of Suntrap, isn't it?"

"Very amusing indeed," agreed Joan.

94

"You see the joke, of course; she can't say a word about the bushes — that's really why she was so annoyed."

Joan nodded and smiled. She was beginning to wonder whether her unexpected visitor was quite right in the head.

"And if you want to rest," he continued, "there's no reason why you shouldn't pull down the blinds."

Joan agreed again. "But, as a matter of fact I never want to," she added gravely, "except in bed of course. I mean there always seems to be so much to do."

"Mother rests a lot," he said, heaving such a profound sigh that his hearer, who was a perspicacious young woman, decided that "Mother" must be extremely tiresome.

"Old people are different, aren't they?" she enquired sweetly.

Her visitor smiled. Perhaps he was thinking how angry his mother would be at hearing herself relegated to this category, but if so he kept his thoughts to himself. "Well, anyhow," he said, "I really just came in to tell you that I thought you were awfully wise to make a clean sweep."

"I'm *so* glad," she nodded — it seemed quite a safe thing to say.

"Yes, sentiment is all very well but it can be overdone — so that's why I came. I'm not supposed to be here at all," he added confidentially. "I'm supposed to be playing golf."

"You — you look like golf."

He surveyed his legs somewhat ruefully — "Horrid things plus fours," he told her.

"Why wear them then?" Joan very naturally enquired.

"Mother likes them. She won't listen when I tell her that I'm too fat for plus fours —"

"You're not fat!"

"I am. I'd like to be tall and lean like Charles. You like Charles, don't you?"

"Yes, of course — don't *you?*" enquired Joan mischievously.

"Nobody could help liking Charles," replied her visitor rather sadly. "He's very good-looking too, isn't he?"

"Very — if you happen to admire that type."

She knew that she was being very naughty, but it was a temptation that she could not resist. The man was like a musical instrument, lying open and ready to respond to the slightest touch of her fingers. He responded now with a pleased and almost incredulous smile. "You don't?" he enquired tentatively.

"Personally," declared Joan. "Personally I *don't* admire that type *very* much. Strong silent soldiers are sometimes — boring. I like men with brains."

He gazed at her, and she could see the thoughts chasing each other through his mind — does she mean me? Have I got brains? No . . . yes . . . perhaps . . . what shall I say?

"I daresay you thought —" he began, "I mean the — the other day when we were here, I expect you thought

I was . . . well . . . pretty *dumb*. I never said a word, did I?"

"You were very silent," Joan agreed.

"I think a lot," he declared boldly, and then, as if terrified by his own boldness, he added wretchedly, "but I'm an awful ass, you know."

"Oh no, don't say that!" cried Joan abandoning her teasing and speaking straight from her tender heart. "Why should you be? Nobody need be. It's dreadful to think *that* about yourself —"

"But I am, yes, I am. You can't help thinking you're an ass if you *are*."

"But you're *not* if you think you are," cried Joan encouragingly. "It's only the people who don't *see* their own silliness who are *really* silly."

He assimilated this profound truth thoughtfully, and Joan, sensing his abstraction, went on with her work. She was very anxious to finish two curtains at least before Jane returned from the village — it was to be a surprise. The machine hummed, and the bees buzzed. The sun shone in at the window upon the fair Miss Fortune's golden curls. Harold Prestcott (for of course it was he) felt a holy peace descend upon him — he had never been so blissfully happy in his life.

CHAPTER
TWELVE

When Jane returned from the village she went round by
the back way to have a look at the devastated area
which had once been a shrubbery and was soon to be a
lawn. She looked at it frequently, not because she liked
looking at it — nobody could — but because when it
was not actually before her eyes she tried to persuade
herself that it couldn't possibly look so frightful as her
recollection evinced. Today, after her visit to Dingleford,
Jane looked at it again and saw that it was even worse
than she had thought. The piles of bushes, their leaves
wilting in the hot sun; the holes from which their
reluctant roots had been torn; the bare sterility of the
trampled earth gave the place an air of indescribable
desolation.

Jane was standing, looking upon the scene with the
deepest pessimism, when the gentle whirr of the sewing
machine fell upon her ears. Her face changed at once
from grave to gay and her eyes danced with mischief.
She put down her basket and crept silently to the
parlour window with the dastardly intention of giving
Joan a fright.

Joan's eyes were fixed upon her work with
praiseworthy concentration, and Harold's eyes were

firmly fixed upon Joan, so neither of them saw the elder Miss Fortune peer in at the leaded casement, and smile, and turn away. (It was well for Harold, no doubt, that he was spared the distress of seeing Miss Fortune outside the window when she was also sitting before him on a chair.)

Leaving her shopping basket in the hall Jane went upstairs to wait until her sister's guest should take his departure. She was in no doubt as to what had happened. Mr. Prestcott had caught Joan unawares, and mistaking her for Jane had not been undeceived — the whole thing was as clear as crystal.

The sisters were accustomed to mistakes of this kind and often used their resemblance with mischievous intent or to further their own ends. Joan did not want her presence at Dingleford to be known, and Jane saw a certain amount of sense in this — not like Nannie who saw no sense in it at all — but Joan must "behave" or else there would be trouble. Supposing Charles came along and found them in the parlour!

This was a surprisingly unpleasant idea to Jane. She sat down in a chair by her bedroom window and considered it in various aspects. Would Charles know? It would be decidedly interesting, of course, to see whether Charles would know the difference between Jane and Joan — rather horrible if he didn't, Jane reflected.

Harold sat and watched Miss Fortune working until it was nearly lunch-time and then, most reluctantly, he took his departure. He walked home through the village with his head in a whirl, thinking about all the astonishing things Miss Fortune had said. "But I *am* fat," he decided sadly, "soft and fat . . . it's frightful . . . what girl could possibly like a fellow who was soft and fat?"

He was passing Mrs. Trail's shop at the moment, and an idea occurred to him which made him pause. He hesitated and then went in. Mrs. Trail was glad to see him for she liked Mr. Prestcott. He was not like the Capting, of course — the Capting, who vanished to foreign parts and returned lean and bronzed and full of glamour to his native place — but still she liked Mr. Prestcott quite a lot.

"Have you — have you got a — a book —" Harold began diffidently.

"A murder story," nodded Mrs. Trail. "I jes' got a new lot in today. Fair 'orrible they looks. Wait an' I'll see —" She crawled under the counter to find them.

But this was not at all what Harold wanted. "A book about — about exercises," he explained, blushing to the roots of his hair.

"Oh, *exercises* — slimmin' I s'pose!" agreed Mrs. Trail understandingly. "Yes, I got one or two — jes' on chance. I thought I might try them myself, but there now, I'm too old I s'pose. The things they tells you to do! Gracious — all tied up in knots, I was, an' stiff for a week! 'Ere you are, Mr. Prestcott, sir."

Harold examined the collection with interest; there were three different pamphlets with instructions and diagrams, and there was also a book on diet for the

100

would-be slim. Harold bought the lot — much to Mrs. Trail's surprise.

"Don't you go an' overdo it, sir," she advised anxiously. "I'd never forgive myself if you was to make yourself ill with them books."

Harold promised to remember her warning; he put the books in his pocket and went on his way with a light heart.

His first idea had been to keep his purpose secret, and to perform his exercises before breakfast on the roof. This was obviously the ideal time and place, not only because all the books were at one in declaring that before breakfast was essential, and the open air was best, but also because his Mother need not know a thing about it. But Harold soon found that secrecy was impracticable, for there was his cold bath (one of the pamphlets was emphatic about a cold bath after exercising) and there was also his diet, which was even more difficult: no puddings, no potatoes, no chocolate creams. Sylvia was distressed beyond measure when Harold refused these familiar delicacies; she conceived the idea that he was bilious and tried to dose him with Gregory's Powder, so the whole thing had to be brought to the light of day.

"But why worry all of a sudden?" she enquired. "You're no fatter than you've always been, and you'll simply hate giving up puddings, won't you?"

"I hate being fat *more*," said Harold firmly.

Sylvia gave in. It was her principle to give in to Harold in small things, and anyhow she was certain that the craze would soon pass. Harold was fond of bed; she could not see him getting up half an hour earlier and contorting his limbs upon the roof, nor did she think that he would hold out long against his favourite puddings — which she was careful to order — and chocolate creams. It would do him no harm to try and fail. Sylvia was wrong on all counts, for with faithful regularity Harold stuck to his regime. He repaired to the roof every morning as the clock struck eight, with the three little books and carried out the graduated exercises which they advised. He described circles with his arms; he touched his toes; he lay on his back and waved his legs in the air; he skipped, and jumped and rolled, and then repaired to the bathroom to take his plunge.

The first few days were somewhat trying — if it had not been for Miss Fortune Harold might easily have relapsed into his comfortable ways — but soon he began to enjoy his morning "do". He found that it put him in splendid fettle for the day. Harold felt fitter, lighter, stronger and more assured, and even, strangely enough, more able to hold his own in moral combat with his mother. Sylvia lived to regret her folly in not putting her foot down firmly at the start.

CHAPTER
THIRTEEN

Joan awoke in the night. It was such an extraordinary occurrence — for she usually slept her ten hours like a contented child — that she sat up and looked at the clock. It was half past twelve. She now saw that her room was filled with a strange red glow, and, skipping out of bed like a kitten, she ran to the window and peered out. The glow was in the sky, it flickered above the treetops, and the dark branches of the trees were outlined against the ruddy light. "It's a *fire!*" said Joan in amazement.

She was wide awake now, thrilled to the core, and her thoughts went straight to Jane who was probably slumbering peacefully through the excitement. Seizing up her dressing-gown she ran to Jane's room and wakened her by bouncing on the bed — a method which cannot be recommended for the nervously inclined.

"What on earth's the matter?" enquired Jane sleepily.

"A fire," Joan whispered. "A raging roaring fire . . . not here, you idiot, away over the trees —"

Jane was wide awake in a moment. They went into Joan's room and looked at it together, leaning out of the window and craning their necks in the effort to see over the trees. There was no doubt about it being a fire, for by this time there was a smell of burning in the air — an acrid smell, quite unmistakeable.

"I believe it's the Manleys' house," said Jane, gazing at the glowing sky with wide eyes. "How awful!"

Who could think of going back to bed, and to sleep, with a raging roaring fire in the vicinity? Not the two Miss Fortunes, that was certain. They dressed quickly, (taking care to make no noise for they were aware that Nannie might not be favourably inclined to the proposed expedition) and putting on dark cloaks with hoods which could be pulled over their heads if necessary, they set off through the woods in the direction of the blaze.

The night was dark and cloudy, and there was a little breeze blowing, it blew straight in their faces as they went along, and on the breeze came the acrid smell, and a strange unnatural warmth, and small pieces of ash sifted through the branches of the trees. They ran and walked and ran again, and soon arrived at the wide-open gates which led to the Manleys' house. Jane had been here before of course, but, even if she had not been here, there would have been no difficulty in finding the way, for the flames lit up the whole scene with a ruddy glow. There was quite a crowd of people here, little groups stood about on the lawn in front of the house, others were hurrying hither and thither carrying silver bowls and boxes and other valuables which they had rescued from the flames. Mr. Manley was standing in the open doorway of his house directing the stream of volunteers in their salvage operations. As to the fire, the whole top storey of the house was ablaze from end to end, flames were spurting from the broken windows like red and yellow tongues, and shooting up from the roof in several places, and there was a strange roaring noise, and a crackling like the sound of newly lighted sticks.

Jane and Joan had been drawn to the scene by the spirit of adventure. They had been pleasantly thrilled by the idea of a fire, but now they were pleasantly thrilled no longer — it was frightful, it was terrifying, it was appalling. They were frozen to the ground with horror at the spectacle.

"It's . . . it's like a wild beast," Joan whispered, clinging to her sister's arm.

Jane agreed. There was something malignant in this element of fire which she had never realised until now. Fire had always been a friend, giving warmth and comfort, but here it was a terrible ravening enemy before whose strength and fury men were powerless. Jane knew that she would never feel the same about fire — tonight had changed her sentiments completely. She would never again look at the dancing flames on the homely hearth with the same comfortable feeling.

They were still standing there when a fire engine drove up at full speed, closely followed by another with a fire escape, and in a few moments the firemen had leapt down and were hard at work. The ladder was reared in the air, the hose was connected with a hydrant in the drive, and a fireman ran up the ladder and began to play a jet of water upon the roof. Hissing steam now added to the other noises of the night, for the heat of the burning house was so great that the water became vapour almost before it reached the flames.

So far, although the whole of Dingleford seemed to be here, nobody had spoken to the Fortune sisters, but now a man passed by carrying a small Dresden cabinet in his arms and Jane saw that it was Charles. She ran forward and caught hold of his coat.

"Charles!" she cried. "Oh, Charles, isn't it frightful? Tell me about it . . . is anybody hurt?"

He put down the cabinet and wiped his face which was streaked with soot. "Hullo!" he said, "No, nobody's hurt, luckily. I've been helping to carry out some of the furniture in the drawing-room . . . I can't stop . . ."

"You mustn't go back," Jane cried, clinging to his arm. "Oh Charles, look — *look*."

The whole roof now seemed to sway and crumble, and great sheets of fire shot through it. A chimney stack wobbled and fell and then the roof disappeared inwards with a crash like thunder. For a moment the fall of the roof dulled the fire — as coal-dross emptied upon a bed of embers dulls the glow — and then the flames shot up skywards higher than before. A moment ago the house had been a burning house, it was now a ruin. The walls still stood, but the roof had gone and the interior was like a furnace.

"That's finished it," Charles said in a low voice. "Thank God they've got everybody out in time."

"The fire engine was useless."

"It was too late. It had gone over to Borrowlands to another fire. This dry weather . . . they don't know how it started . . . it was hopeless, really, from the very first."

"You won't go back," Jane pleaded.

"It wouldn't be any use," he agreed. "Let's sit down for a minute, shall we."

They sat down on the dry grass and watched the activities of the firemen. Now that the roof had gone, and the walls were crumbling, it was easier to control the flames. The house was absolutely wrecked but there was less danger of the fire spreading to the outbuildings.

For a time Charles and Jane were silent, for the scene was so distracting that they could think of nothing else, but after a little Charles remembered that he was going away tomorrow, and would not see Jane for days. He remembered also the last time he had seen Jane and how queerly she had behaved.

"Have I done anything — anything you don't like?" he enquired at last, seizing the bull by the horns.

Jane turned and looked at him in surprise. Her face was irradiated by the glow of the fire, and the surprise upon it was unmistakeable.

"I thought you were fed up about something," Charles explained, "and that man with the patent leather . . . I mean the fellow in the sports car . . . I mean I wondered who he was."

"Oh, that was Jack," said Jane, her face clearing. "He's a friend of my sister's."

Charles was delighted at this news. "Then it's all right?" he said eagerly.

"Of course it's all right," nodded Jane.

"I told you I was going to London, didn't I?" Charles continued. "Mother's lawyer wants to see me, and I've got to go to the War House about something, but I'll see you when I come back."

"I shan't run away," said Jane laughing.

While Charles and Jane were thus clearing away the slight misunderstanding which had arisen between them Joan was having some small adventures of her own. She had wandered round to the back of the house to see what was going on there, and had encountered several people who seemed to know her, and were quite ready to talk to her and tell her the whole history of the conflagration. It was more comfortable on this side of the house, for the wind was carrying the heat and the ashes in the other direction. She was standing on a piece of wall, surveying the scene with interest when she was accosted by a gentleman with a round red face and somewhat shaggy grey hair. He was clad in clerical garments, and was carrying a silver teapot under one arm and a silver coffee-pot under the other.

"Good evening, Miss Fortune," he observed. "This is a sad scene, is it not?"

Joan came down off her perch. "Not *sad*," she replied, smiling at the clergyman in a friendly manner. "I mean you couldn't describe it as sad, really."

"How would you describe it then?" he enquired somewhat taken aback at her temerity.

"I would say it was frightful, horrifying, thrilling or terrifying," declared Joan promptly, "but I wouldn't say it was sad. You see if a thing is sad it gives you a lump in your throat, but this fire gives you shivers up your spine — that's the difference."

Mr. Ruff was more used to giving instruction than to receiving it, so he was surprised and not altogether pleased to find the roles reversed. "I still maintain that it is sad," he declared. "This fine old house reduced to a heap of ashes, and the Manleys homeless — to me the situation seems intensely sad," and so saying he walked away.

Joan saw that she had blundered, and she was sorry for her sins. I'm awful, she thought, I really *am* awful. Jane will be furious with me for offending the poor old thing — perhaps I'd better find Jane before I do any more mischief.

But to find Jane was easier said than done, for Jane had suddenly decided that she must find Joan, and the two sisters wandered round looking for each other for some time before they finally met face to face under the archway which led into the stable yard. Dozens of people had seen them during their peregrinations, and some of the more mentally alert had registered the impression that Miss Fortune was amazingly ubiquitous — indeed she seemed to be everywhere at once — but as nobody had actually seen the two sisters together their secret remained intact.

Dawn was breaking over the hills to the eastward when Jane and Joan wound their way home through the woods.

"I'm glad we went," Joan said thoughtfully. "I'm sorry about the house of course, but, if it had to burn — well, I'm glad I was there to see it happen. It was terrific, wasn't it?"

Jane felt the same, it was an experience she would not have missed, but she was glad to be on her way home, for she was so tired and cold that her teeth were chattering in her head.

They let themselves into the cottage as quietly as mice, and scuttled up the stairs to bed. Nannie was still sleeping the sleep of the just quite oblivious to all the excitement.

CHAPTER
FOURTEEN

The morning after the fire Jane Fortune awoke to find her throat tickly, and her head aching. She sneezed five times in succession with frightful violence, but far from clearing her stuffy nose the paroxysm added to her discomfort.

Nannie, summoned to the bedside, took her temperature and found it to be 99.2°. "You'll stay where you are, Miss Jane," she said firmly. "It's one of your nasty colds beginning. Dear knows where you've got it?"

Jane could have enlightened her, but it seemed unnecessary, she signified her willingness to remain where she was in nasal tones — indeed she had no desire to rise and go about her daily business for she felt quite ill.

"Miss Joan'll 'ave to do the shoppin'," Nannie continued. "I've got me 'ands full at 'ome without trailin' to the village an' back."

Joan was sitting on the end of the bed — she was not in the least afraid of catching cold from the patient for she was practically immune from these annoying afflictions. She looked at Nannie and nodded. "I'll go," she said.

"That's all right then," declared Nannie, her face brightening at the news. "I'll just make out the list — you don't need to worry your head about that Frenchy, Miss Joan, and just you say to Mrs. Trail that you're Miss Fortune's sister come to stay."

Joan winked at Jane. She had no intention of saying who she was — it would be quite unnecessary.

Now that this important question was settled, Nannie unbent. "I've got a bit of news for you," she declared. "It was Mr. Fawkes the postman told me — a 'orrible thing 'appened last night."

"What happened?" Joan enquired, gazing at Nannie with large innocent eyes.

"The Manleys' 'ouse was burnt to the ground," declared Nannie dramatically. She was so thrilled by her own announcement that she failed to observe the lack of surprise shown by her audience. "Yes," she continued, "the 'ole place was burnt to ashes . . . a beam in the kitchen chimbley caught fire. Land Sakes, I 'ope nothin' like that 'appens 'ere! These old 'ouses are dangerous — so Mr. Fawkes says. We've 'ad a flood already. Fancy the 'ole place burnin' down like that an' us in our beds not knowin' a thing about it!"

"Fancy!" said Joan wickedly.

"Nobody was burnt," Nannie continued, "an' that was lucky, it was the dogs barkin' what warned them. Mr. Giles Manley woke up an' smelt fire, an' they all got out in time. It was a n'orful blaze, Mr. Fawkes says, an' all Dingleford was there — more fools they — I wouldn't miss my night's sleep for all the fires in Christendom."

112

The twins were quite glad to hear this, for they had felt a trifle guilty in not giving Nannie a chance to see the show. It had seemed a little selfish, somehow, and whatever faults they had, selfishness was entirely absent from their natures.

"*That's* all right then," said Joan, voicing her relief.

"What's all right?" enquired Nannie suspiciously, but she got no satisfactory reply.

Jane's cold ran its horrible course — for three days she sneezed and slept, and slept and sneezed — and for three days Joan took her place, sallying forth to the village to do the shopping. The weather, which had been fine and dry for so long had now broken, but Joan did not mind the rain. She put on her waterproof, and a black sou-wester, and the galoshes which Jane had bought from Mrs. Trail came in very useful. It was so wet that very few people were about the village, but Joan took care to bow to anybody who showed an interest in her, and was very pleasant to Mrs. Ruff the vicar's wife who pursued her across the village green and asked her to come to a meeting at the church hall to arrange about the annual bazaar.

"Of course I'll come. It will be lovely," Joan declared, smiling mischievously at the thought of how Jane would enjoy the treat.

Mrs. Ruff was charmed. Her task of whipping up the residents of Dingleford to attend the Bazaar Meeting was a hateful one — nobody wanted to come — they all knew that if they attended the meeting they were sure to be saddled with a "stall". Sometimes they were able to think of a plausible excuse, and sometimes they agreed to come with ungracious reluctance — they never accepted the invitation with smiling alacrity as Miss Fortune had done.

"So sweet of you!" purred Mrs. Ruff.

"Not at all . . . a pleasure," declared Joan.

Mrs. Ruff was all the more surprised at Miss Fortune's charm in view of the lamentable account of her which had been given at the family breakfast table. "A dreadfully pert girl — rude and unmannerly," had been the vicar's dictum delivered with most unusual warmth. But Mrs. Ruff saw no signs of pertness in Miss Fortune, and her manners could not be bettered. Mrs. Ruff wished that the other residents of Dingleford were half as nice.

"I must come and see you," she declared. "I would have come before, but the children have had chickenpox — there are so many things I want to talk to you about."

"Oh do come — come to tea," cried Joan cordially, and then remembering Jane's cold, and having no wish to entertain Mrs. Ruff herself, she added, "Come *next* week — I shall be *quite* settled by then."

They parted on most amicable terms.

Joan was not really "a country girl", she preferred streets and shops to country lanes, but there was something about Dingleford which attracted her. She liked the long road to the village which wound along by the side of the Dingle because there was such a lot to see — so many different trees and flowers and birds whose like she had never before encountered.

114

Sometimes she stood and watched the stream as it swept past — brown and turbid with the rains — and wondered where it had come from and where it was going. It was going to the sea eventually, of course, but the sea was a long way off and it would pass all sorts of interesting places before it arrived at its destination. The Dingle reminded Joan of a poem which she had learnt long ago when she was quite a little girl and had delivered with fine effect at the School Concert.

"'I come from haunt of coot and herne,'" said Joan slowly, but she could remember no more. It was all about a river which went on for ever — just like the Dingle. Although she could not remember the poem, she remembered very clearly that it was really Jane's "piece" but Jane had been too shy to stand up and say it before everybody in the school hall. So after Joan had sung her song — a cradle song it was — she and Jane had retired to the bathroom together and exchanged bows and sashes (the marks of identity insisted upon by bewildered teachers) and had returned to the hall disguised as each other — Jane in Joan's pink ribbons and Joan in Jane's blue — so that the more dashing Joan could take her twin's place when the time for recitation arrived.

Joan had not thought of this for years, it was the Dingle that had brought it all back — the Dingle rushing along so impatiently between its high banks. These banks were pitted with rabbit holes, and covered with a tangle of brambles, and there were willows whose long graceful branches bent over and trailed in the brown water, catching little sticks in their fingers,

115

and pieces of hay. Further on, nearer the village, the willows had been cut, and the banks were gay with wild flowers whose faces had been washed by the rain. At the ford, which was quite near Mrs. Trail's shop, the stream widened, and the banks were flat and gravelly, and Joan stood and wondered who had crossed the river here — horsemen, stage-coaches, post-chaises — it was frightfully interesting to think of it.

The village itself was a delightful spot, so Joan decided. It wore a leisurely air and there was no overcrowding, for the old gabled cottages were separated from their neighbours by gardens, and from their vis-à-vis by the broad space of the village-green. The trees which stood upon this green space were heavy with foliage, and when the sun shone through the thick blanket of grey cloud — as it did now and then — and a small breeze wandered up the valley, the old trees shook themselves gently and each one had a thunder-shower of its very own — a thunder-shower of rainbow hued diamonds.

It was far too wet for the work in the shrubbery to continue and Charles did not appear at the cottage — he had gone to London of course — but Harold Prestcott, true to his promise, dropped in to mend the bell. He called one afternoon when Joan was out, and she returned from her walk to find him there.

Nannie met her at the door with an anxious face. "I didn't know what to say," she hissed. "That young Mr. Prestcott's 'ere. I said Miss Jane was out — whatever shall we do?"

"*Who* is it?" Joan enquired.

"That young Mr. Prestcott — *you* know, Miss Joan — the people the 'ouse belonged to before us . . . a nice spoken young gentleman . . . said 'e'd promised to mend the bell."

Joan's face cleared. "Oh yes . . . yes, so that's who he is!" she exclaimed.

" 'E's mending it ever so nice," declared Nannie complacently. "I must say the young gentlemen of Dingleford are clever an' useful — there was Capting Weatherby 'alf drowned in the cistern, an' now Mr. Prestcott at the bell."

"*Who* was drowned in the cistern?" cried Joan in amazement — was this yet another of Jane's young men?

" '*Alf* drowned, I said," declared Nannie. "We dried 'im up all right."

Joan was about to enquire further into the matter when Harold emerged from the pantry in his shirt sleeves followed by a fat black pug. His eyes widened when he saw Miss Fortune. "Oh, you're back!" he said.

It was not a very brilliant remark, but Joan understood the underlying meaning. "Are you glad?" she enquired, smiling at him brazenly.

"Glad! Of course I'm glad. I came to see you didn't I?" cried Harold. He was somewhat alarmed to hear the bold words issue from his lips, but, far from being annoyed, Miss Fortune seemed pleased.

"Come along and talk to me then," she said laughing. "Is tea in the parlour, Nannie?"

They went into the parlour with Francesca at their heels and the door was shut.

Nannie was somewhat shocked at Miss Joan's "forwardness" with Mr. Prestcott. She was an old-fashioned woman and disapproved of modern ways. Miss Joan was a minx — there was no other word for it — and, later, when the gentleman had gone, Nannie would give her a talking to. In the meantime there was nothing to be done, for the tea was already laid, and as there were two cups on the tray she had no excuse to enter the room, so, after listening at the door for a few moments to the murmur of conversation — not a word of which could be distinguished — she heaved a sigh and retired to the kitchen to get on with her work.

Joan was aware of Nannie's disapproval, but also of her impotence. She led Harold into the parlour and proceeded to give him tea. She had already decided that she liked Harold a good deal. "We can talk now," said Joan, smiling at him engagingly.

Unfortunately Harold was shy again and could find nothing to say to the adorable creature. He was so miserable that he almost wished himself back at Suntrap having tea with his Mother in the drawing room. Francesca's behaviour did not help matters at all, for she had taken a tremendous fancy to Miss Fortune and insisted on snuffling round Miss Fortune's legs, and even leapt upon her knee — an attention which Miss Fortune showed no signs of enjoying.

"Down Francesca, down," cried Harold, and he smacked Francesca's nose which surprised and hurt her considerably, for she was used to people liking her — or at least pretending that they did.

"I don't like dogs," said Joan with complete frankness, "but the odd thing is they seem to like me."

"Francesca is spoilt," said Harold apologetically.

Francesca now retired under the writing table in high dudgeon at the unusual and brutal treatment she had received. She expected to be pursued with apologies and endearments, and was quite ready to be friends again in consideration for a piece of that nice rich chocolate cake which she saw on the cakestand, but nobody troubled about her any more.

"It *was* clever of you to mend the bell," Joan said.

"No it wasn't," replied Harold earnestly. "It's just that I know its ways. If it goes wrong again just send for me."

"But it would be such a bother."

"No bother at all. I often come this way after tea — just for a walk and to exercise Francesca. I rather like looking at the new bridge after the workmen have gone. You know I really wanted to be an engineer," he added with a burst of confidence.

"Why aren't you, then?" she enquired, and then, when he was still looking for a reply, she added "*What* are you, Mr. Prestcott?"

"I'm nothing," replied Harold bitterly, "just a fool, that's all."

"Naughty," said Miss Fortune, "I told you that you weren't to say that, didn't I?"

Harold agreed that she had. "You make me feel as if I could do things," he added thoughtfully. "I can *talk* to you."

"Can't you talk to other people?"

"No, I can't," he declared. "I get all hot and bothered — it's dreadful really."

"It must be dreadful," Miss Fortune agreed.

"You know," said Harold thoughtfully, "you know that first day when I saw you when I called with Mother? Well, it's really most awfully queer, but I didn't think that you were so — so —"

"Pretty?" enquired Miss Fortune with a pleased and interested expression.

"No — I mean yes, you were just as pretty. In fact I thought I had never seen anybody so pretty before," said Harold boldly, "but, somehow, I didn't feel . . . it's so difficult to explain . . . I didn't feel . . ."

Miss Fortune seemed to understand. She smiled and nodded and pressed her guest to more tea, and was quite distressed when he refused a piece of chocolate cake — it was because of the diet of course.

Their talk drifted along very pleasantly, and they spoke of the fire — how dreadful it had been, but rather exciting too — and Miss Fortune voiced her sympathy with the Manleys in the destruction of their home.

"But they don't mind a bit," Harold told her. "At least I suppose Mr. Manley minds, but the others are delighted. You see it was an ugly house — there was something horrible about it."

"Was it haunted?" asked Miss Fortune with wide eyes.

"Not exactly — not haunted by a ghost — but there was something evil about it. Giles could explain it to you if you want to know. They're going to live in London now — at any rate until they have built a new house for themselves — and I'm sure they'll all be much happier there."

"They've gone to London already, haven't they?" Miss Fortune enquired — she had heard this piece of local news from Mrs. Trail.

"Yes, they've gone. Giles and Erica are coming to stay with us for the dance. They wouldn't like to miss *that*, you see."

Miss Fortune was about to ask, "What dance?" for she was inordinately fond of dancing, when her guest leapt to his feet with an exclamation of dismay.

"Look at the time!" he cried, "Oh Goodness, I must fly! Mother was expecting me home at five."

"She won't mind," Miss Fortune prophesied, comfortingly, but far from correctly. "You can just tell her that you were mending the bell for me."

"Hm'm," said Harold doubtfully. He had no intention of offering any such excuse, for he was well aware that it would have no soothing effect upon his Mother.

CHAPTER
FIFTEEN

At this very moment when Harold was taking leave of Miss Fortune, a tall broad shouldered man with a voluminous check coat and a soft hat might have been seen entering the bar at the Cat and Fiddle. Mr. Widgett was getting ready for the evening rush; he was polishing glasses and setting them in a neat phalanx upon the polished counter. His bald head was rosy and his pale blue eyes were slightly protuberant with the exertion of his work.

"Zis bar, is 'e open?" enquired the newcomer in careful broken English.

" 'E is — I mean it is," declared Mr. Widgett blandly.

"You 'ave beer 'ere?"

"Lor'!" exclaimed Mr. Widgett. "I shouldn't get far if I didn't 'ave beer, should I? Wot d'yer think this is — a milk bar?"

"Zis is a meelk bar?" enquired the stranger, frowning with the effort to understand.

"That's right!" said Mr. Widgett, winking significantly.

"Zen I cannot 'ave beer —" he stopped suddenly on perceiving that a large gloss of frothing ale was standing beside him on the counter.

"Is that right?" Mr. Widgett enquired.

"Ah! I see! I do not onnerstan'," announced the man, his eyes gleaming at the welcome sight. "I sink you say 'Zis is a meelk bar' — ha ha!"

"Ha, ha, ha!" echoed Mr. Widgett, "that's good, that is."

The stranger had taken three quarters of the pint in one draught, he put down the glass and smiled. "Yes, yes, zat's good!" he declared. "You 'ave good meelk 'ere, Mistaire Cat an' Feedle."

Mr. Widgett explained carefully that "Cat and Fiddle" was the name of his house, not himself, but, as his English was extremely racy and colloquial, and the stranger's English of the text book variety, they did not get much further. They laughed a good deal, and more beer was ordered and paid for, and pleasant relations were established.

"You 'ave been 'ere long time — yes?" enquired the stranger at last.

"Yes," said Widgett, nodding his head energetically and speaking very loud indeed as if his customer were deaf.

"You know all ze peoples round about 'ere — yes?"

"Yes," replied Widgett again, nodding more violently than before.

"Good. You know all ze peoples. You know per'aps Mees Fortune — yes?"

"Well, in a manner of speakin' I knows 'er, an' in a manner of speakin' I doesn't," declared Mr. Widgett solemnly.

This was far beyond the stranger's comprehension. He gazed at the innkeeper hopelessly. "Zis English, mon Dieu!" he exclaimed. "I will nevaire know 'im — nevaire."

"I've seen 'er," Widgett continued, almost shouting in the effort to make the man understand. "I've 'eard about 'er, an' I've seen 'er, but I 'aven't never spoke to 'er — see? Ladies doesn't come 'ere much — not being a milk bar."

"Ha ha! Our good joke again!" cried the man genially. "You will give me a leetle more of zat good meelk of yours — yes — I 'ave a beeg — a 'ow you say — *soif?* Ah, zat's right. Now zen, zis Mees Fortune — she 'ave a leetle sistaire stayin' wis 'er — yes?"

"No," said Mr. Widgett shaking his head. "No, not as I've 'eard — an I 'ears most things. She 'as 'er old Nannie — p'raps that's wot you mean —"

"No, no! It is a young sistaire — young an', oh so bee-oo-ti-ful — now zen, you 'ave seen 'er . . . yes?"

"No," said Mr. Widgett loudly. "No. She's a good looker 'erself but she 'ain't got no sister — NO."

The stranger sighed gustily. "See 'ere," he said. "It is my secret I tell you . . . so nice, so *convenable* you are. Zis young sistaire of Mees Fortune, she is a grreat frien' of me, an' I buy 'er a leetle present for 'er burseday . . . see? I come 'ere all ze way from London to give 'er zis present. Now zen, she is 'ere . . . yes?"

"No," said Mr. Widgett sadly. "No, she ain't 'ere. I'd say 'yes' like a shot if it would do you any good, but there it is — *she ain't 'ere.* You've 'ad a wild goose chase, that's what."

"Ha ha!" I chase after ze wild goose, yes . . . or per'aps ze wild swan . . . ze bee-oo-ti-ful wild swan . . .

124

ah, *quelle dommage* . . . what a tousand peeties! Za leetle wild swan will not 'ave 'er burseday present on ze right day."

Mr. Widgett was extremely sorry about it, for he was a good-natured man. He racked his brains for a way out of the dilemma and eventually suggested that Miss Fortune should be visited and asked for her sister's address. She would be sure to know, of course, and would be only too ready to oblige. Mr. Widgett was enchanted with the plan but his customer raised innumerable objections. They argued quite heatedly for a few minutes — all the more heatedly because of the language difficulty which increased when they became excited. They were still arguing when the door opened and Harold Prestcott walked in with Francesca under his arm.

For the last few days, since he had started his rigid diet, he had made a habit of calling in at the Cat and Fiddle on his way home from his evening walk. He found that a pint of Widgett's beer filled up an empty space inside him which had previously been filled with cake and chocolate creams. The diet allowed an occasional glass of beer, but Sylvia Prestcott had refused to provide it — beer was "low", it was mixed up with betting in Sylvia's mind — she was dreadfully old fashioned in this.

Widgett welcomed Harold with open arms. "There now," he exclaimed. "Ain't that lucky! 'E'res a young gentleman can tell you wot you wants ter know. You ask 'im."

The big man swung round and looked at Harold, he saw a young gentleman with a pug under one arm and sized him up with keen scrutiny. The young gentleman had a round pleasant face — he looked diffident, soft, just a trifle foolish; he looked, in fact, the very man for the purpose. If this young gentleman knew anything it would be quite easy to make him talk. With a beaming smile he offered Harold a drink and proceeded to pump him forthwith.

"You are acquainted wis Mees Fortune . . . yes? Ah, zat is nice. Now you will tell me . . . it will be so vairy kind an' *convenable* . . . she 'as a leetle sistaire stayin' wis 'er, yes?"

"No, she hasn't," replied Harold with conviction. "I know her quite well — in fact I've just been to see her — and her sister isn't there."

"She tell you, per'aps, zat 'er sistaire come an' stay soon?" suggested the stranger anxiously.

"No, her sister is in London. I know all about it because the house belonged to us, you see. She told my mother all her plans."

"I not unnerstan'," declared the stranger frowning.

Harold could have explained the whole thing quite easily in French, for he was fluent in several modern languages (having been abroad with his mother when most boys are learning Latin at school) but he was much too shy to converse with the man in his own tongue. It would seem rather rude, Harold thought; it would seem as if he thought that he could speak French better than the man could speak English. He could, of course, there was no doubt of it, but that was not the

126

point. Harold stood the man a drink in return for the one that the man had stood *him*, and they conversed haltingly, foggily, for several minutes before Harold departed on his way home.

CHAPTER
SIXTEEN

Jane's cold was much better next day and her temperature was "down to normal." It was the day of the Golf Club Dance.

"You can't go," Nannie declared. "It's madness to think of it — gettin' up out of your bed an' gallivantin' off to a dance! I'd 'ave you on my 'ands with pew-monia. Besides, look what a sight you are!" she added unfeelingly.

Jane murmured feebly that she did not want to go to the beastly dance, she felt rotten and it was just her luck to miss all the fun.

"Dance, indeed!" snorted Nannie.

"Dance!" cried Joan, who had entered with her sister's lunch tastefully arranged upon a tray. "Dance! Who said 'dance'? What dance? When is it?"

Jane explained languidly that it was the Golf Club Dance, that it was taking place tonight at the Club House and that she was supposed to be going as Colonel Staunton's guest.

"I'll go instead," said Joan firmly.

Nannie threw up her hands in dismay — "I arsk you!" she cried. "Whatever next? That's what I'd like to know — *whatever* next?"

Joan did not reply, she took a few steps across the floor and pirouetted lightly, while she hummed the first few bars of "My Boy Can Dance". Jane watched indulgently from the bed and thought how pretty she was and reflected — with justifiable complacency — that, as she herself was exactly like Joan, she must be quite as pretty. The conclusion was perfectly reasonable and mathematically sound.

It is given to few people to see themselves as others see them, and even fewer people would be pleased, as Jane was, at the sight.

"Why should'ett she go," said Jane in nasal tones. "I beed dobody would dow it wassett be."

"Lamb!" cried Joan. "Dear darling lamb! I'll be as good as gold."

"You don't know 'ow!" Nannie told her "The way you were carrying on with young Mr. Prestcott —"

"I'll tell you all about it when I come back," continued Joan excitedly. "I won't do anything — well anything mischievous, you know. Oh Jane, it will be lovely!"

There was a little argument about it, but not much, for Nannie, in her inmost heart, liked her "children" to enjoy themselves, and she simply loved seeing them in their pretty frocks and fussing about their hair. So when Joan cooed, "Nannie darling, you'll do my hair won't you? I know you will," her heart melted completely and she cast caution and discretion to the winds.

By eight o'clock Jane was much better, her head had cleared and she felt more like herself, so was able to take a proprietary interest in the dressing of her substitute.

"Will you dress in my room, so that I can see you?" she asked.

Joan was delighted to oblige.

Dressing was a serious business, of course. First of all she undressed; then she seized her curls and twisted them up in a knob on the top of her head. Most women would have looked frightful but it was impossible for Joan to look other than ravishing. Indeed her small clearly cut features seemed more delicately chiselled than ever and the pure line of her neck and ear was displayed in all its beauty when bereft of the usual cluster of golden curls.

After this came the bath, from which she returned, rosy and scented, and, casting her blue silk dressing gown on the floor, she proceeded to array herself in the scantiest and filmiest of underwear imaginable.

"Darling," said Jane, "Darling, I simply can't believe I look so lovely!"

"Darling pet-lamb, of course you do," returned Joan, pausing for a moment in the act of drawing up her stocking, to kiss her hand to her double in the bed.

Joan was now ready for her frock. She ran off to her own little room and returned a few minutes later clad in a straight-cut dress of scarlet broche. It was high in front — almost up to her throat — but the back was completely nonexistent.

Nannie, who had arrived on the scenes to do her hair, cried out in horror at the sight. "My Gracious, Miss Joan! You ain't never going out in that dress! *No*, an' that's my last word. It may be all very well for London . . . but 'ere — NO."

"I think it is a little bit —" Jane began.

"But I haven't got anything else fit to *wear*," wailed Joan. "Nothing, absolutely nothing except my black, and my silver . . . my white's *filthy* . . ."

"Then you'll wear Miss Jane's pink net," said Nannie promptly.

"But Nannie —"

"Or you won't go at all. Take your choice."

Joan took her choice. She divested herself of the scarlet broche and allowed Nannie to slip the pink net frock over her head. The change in her appearance was amazing.

"I look like a deb," said Joan a trifle regretfully as she surveyed herself in the full length mirror which was screwed to the wall.

"And that's all to the good," Nannie declared, "for you'll be more likely to be'ave yourself. It's a pretty dress."

It was pretty and it became Joan well. The bodice was of pink satin, quite plain save for a silver rose on one shoulder; the skirt was of pink net, rather full and stiff, it stood out from her slim waist and reached almost to the floor.

Joan was all ready, prinked and powdered and her golden curls in trim order, long before the scheduled time and with many admonitions to stay quiet and not crush herself, Nannie hurried away to finish her ironing.

"You'd better tell me about everybody," Joan said, perching carefully on the end of her sister's bed. "I shall get into a most awful mess if you don't."

"Colonel Staunton is pink and fat," said Jane thoughtfully. "I wouldn't *sit out* with him if I were you —"

"Oh, that sort!" nodded Joan.

"He can take you in to supper," Jane continued, "and you'll have to dance with him once or twice. Then there's the Wickhams — two brothers, with long pale faces and sticking out teeth — you can't mistake them. Giles Manley is tall and dark . . . he's very keen on dancing, so he probably dances well. Don't forget to be nice to Mrs. Prestcott if she's there."

"What's she like?"

"Tall and willowy, white face and dark eyes," said Jane promptly. "She's got a son —"

"I know Harold —"

"*Wet*," declared Jane.

"Oh no, I like Harold," exclaimed Joan impulsively. "He's sweet when you really get to know him . . . a little shy, of course at times, but —"

"There's no accounting for tastes."

Joan said no more about Harold, she was quite glad that Jane did not appreciate him at his true worth. By an easily discernable association of ideas she passed on to Charles.

"What am I to do about Charles?" she asked, a trifle slyly. "I suppose you want me to be *very* nice to him."

"He isn't going," said Jane. She was staring at the ceiling with a somewhat inscrutable expression and there was a little secret smile twitching the corners of her mouth.

Joan had a sudden strong conviction that if Charles had been going to the dance Jane would have been much less resigned to the prospect of staying at home. She pursed up her lips and emitted a soft whistle — a most unladylike proceeding it was.

"Don't be silly," said Jane.

"There's no accounting for tastes," Joan reminded her, grinning. "Don't worry Jane, I haven't much use for that pukkha sahib type. We're both delighted that the gallant captain won't be there —"

"Then there's Mr. Ruff, the vicar," continued Jane, paying no attention to the playful badinage, "and his brother-in-law — I liked him; and there's Erica Manley and Mr. Ames. You had better look out for Erica — she's a queer fish — rather dangerous —"

"Stop!" cried Joan, laughing and putting her fingers in her ears. "Stop for Goodness Sake! I shall never remember all these people. How on earth did you manage to collect such a host of acquaintances in one short month?"

They talked a little longer and then Joan went downstairs, she was so excited that it was difficult to sit still, and there was still ten minutes, perhaps longer, before Colonel Staunton could be expected to call. She went into the parlour and turned on the wireless to pass the time. "An anticyclone is approaching the British Isles and a ridge of high pressure —" began the pleasant soothing voice of the announcer.

Joan had no sooner left the room than Jane began to think of at least a dozen things which she ought to have told her. There was Erica, for instance. "I should have told her what Erica was *like*," said Jane frowning to herself at her own foolishness. "Erica will speak to her and she won't know who it is or anything. Oh dear!" She hesitated for a few moments and then made up her mind. Two white feet (which Mrs. Trail had observed to be small and shapely) slid out of bed and groped for the blue mules which were lying on the floor.

Colonel Staunton was standing upon the doorstep of Dingleford Cottage, wondering what to do. He had pealed the bell till he was tired, but the wires had got stuck again. Like everybody in Dingleford, Colonel Staunton was aware of the idiosyncrasies of this bell; it was by no means the first time that it had failed to respond to his assault.

"I can't stand here all night," said the Colonel to himself. "Damn it all, we'll be late."

To be late was unthinkable, for he was bred to military punctuality, so after one more strenuous, but wholly ineffectual pull, he opened the door and walked into the hall.

Miss Fortune was coming downstairs, (she was on the bottom step to be exact) and the Colonel saw her at once. He started forward eagerly and then paused. Miss Fortune (he now perceived) was clad in pyjamas and a blue silk dressing gown; her bare feet were thrust into mules, her golden curls confined in a pale blue net . . . it was an unusual style of dress for a lady who was going to a dance, and the Colonel, whose brain worked slowly, gazed at her with his mouth open.

Miss Fortune gazed back, horror-stricken at the unexpected meeting and then turned and fled upstairs like the wind.

Colonel Staunton waited for a few moments, gathering his wits. There were only two explanations of the incident: either Miss Fortune had forgotten that this was THE NIGHT or else she was one of those annoying females who have no idea of time, and are late — hours late — for every appointment. The whole thing was very annoying and Colonel Staunton was annoyed. He decided that he *must* find somebody and ascertain what was the meaning of it, so he looked round the hall, selected a likely looking door and opened it boldly. It was the door leading into the kitchen and there was Nannie ironing on the kitchen table and humming to herself — as usual a trifle flat.

"Laws!" exclaimed Nannie.

The Colonel marched in and placed his opera hat on the table. He intended to have a thorough explanation of everything, but first his own, somewhat unconventional entrance must be cleared up. "I rang," he began, in a loud booming voice, "but the bell appears to be out of action —"

"It's always goin' wrong, sir," Nannie assured him. "I'll run an' get 'er this minute." She took off her ironing apron and flung it on a chair. "She's all ready, sir," added Nannie smiling at him confidentially.

"She is not," declared the Colonel.

"What?"

"I have just seen her. She was in her — ahem — night attire."

"My Gracious!" exclaimed Nannie in dismay — a dismay caused by the fact that she realised exactly what had happened; it was Miss Jane he had seen, of course, Miss Jane wandering about the house with her cold and all — "pew-monia," thought Nannie, "that'll be the end of it."

Colonel Staunton saw the dismay, and gave it his own meaning. He became less angry when he found that Nannie was his ally and sympathiser. "Yes," he said, nodding solemnly. "She isn't *nearly* ready. You had better go and see what's what."

"I will do," Nannie promised. "She won't be five minutes —"

"Won't she?" enquired the Colonel with bitter sarcasm. "I know more about women — five minutes indeed! I'll eat my hat if she's ready in twenty five."

The words had hardly left his lips and Nannie was still trying to find a soothing reply, when the kitchen door opened and Miss Fortune stood before him in all her glory. She was a radiant vision, curled, scented and powdered, her pink frock moulding her pretty figure and swinging gracefully from her slender waist. To say that Joan was surprised to find her escort hob-nobbing with Nannie in the kitchen would be to understate the case. Her eyes widened and her mouth opened but no sound came from between her lips. The Colonel was even more amazed, but he was so enchanted by the beauty of the vision before him that he did not pause to consider how impossible the transformation was. He

136

gazed at the vision and the vision gazed back. Nannie flung herself into the breach with admirable presence of mind —

" 'Ere you are at last, Miss!" she cried. " 'Ere's the Colonel been waitin' for you I-don'-know-'ow-long, an' you careering about the 'ouse in your dressin'-gown —"

"Me!" exclaimed Miss Fortune in amazement.

"Yes, *you*," declared Nannie, nodding and becking significantly behind the Colonel's back. "You, *careering about in your dressin' gown* . . . but never mind . . . you're ready now."

"Charming!" murmured the Colonel vaguely. "Delightful . . . charming . . . beautiful . . . an English Rose!"

By this time Joan had arrived at the conclusion that somehow or other — heaven alone knew how — the Colonel must have encountered Jane wandering about in pyjamas. It was absolutely necessary that he should not be allowed to *brood* upon it. It was absolutely necessary that his mind should be "taken off" the subject. She swept forward with a dazzling smile. "Have I been *ages?*" she asked. "How naughty of me not to be ready when you came! You *will* forgive me, won't you?"

"Not at all," he declared. "Delighted . . . charmed . . . you've been extremely quick . . . I mean . . . I don't understand it at all . . . I mean I don't know how you managed it," but Miss Fortune was smiling at him, and her little white hand was in his. What did it matter if he could not understand? Nothing mattered except that she was here and he was going to take her to the dance.

Nannie watched the scene with mingled feelings. She could not but be pleased at the havoc wrought upon the gallant Colonel by the charms which she had helped to enhance, but Miss Joan was a minx all the same. "She didn't ought to do that to the pore old gentleman," said Nannie to herself.

"Come along, then," said Miss Fortune. "We mustn't be late, must we?"

He followed her like a somnambulist and Nannie had to run after him with his hat which he had left upon her kitchen table. She could not help chuckling as she pressed it into his nerveless hands, for the temptation to remind him that he was sworn to eat it was almost irresistible.

CHAPTER
SEVENTEEN

The club-house was decorated with flowers and flags and filled with a chattering throng of people bent upon enjoyment. Miss Fortune pushed her way into the Ladies' Cloak Room and found about six women skirmishing for the single mirror, powder puff in hand. A tall girl in green chiffon with a beautiful bare back seemed to be taking up more than her fair share of space. She was exactly like a Vogue picture — smart and sophisticated. This was exactly the type of girl which Joan admired, and her thoughts sped to the scarlet broche frock which was now lying disconsolately over the back of a chair. Nannie is so *silly*, she thought, so frightfully old fashioned — I could easily have worn it tonight, and then I should have looked like that girl instead of like a baby at a children's party.

"Erica *dear!*" said somebody in a plaintive tone. "When you've *quite* finished with the mirror —"

"Patience is a virtue — as Mr. Ames would say," declared the green girl outlining her pretty mouth with the latest shade of scarlet lipstick.

So that's Erica, is it! said Joan to herself, and I've got to look out for her because she's a queer fish — and dangerous. I wish I'd found out more about her.

"Yes, I'm all new," Erica was declaring, in response to an enquiry about her frock (she was doing her eyes now, so speech was easier). "Every stitch I possessed was burnt."

"How awful!" somebody sympathised.

"Not awful at all . . . *lovely*. You can't think how lovely it is to start fresh like that — from the skin upwards."

"We must have a fire!" laughed another girl. "How does one start a fire, Erica?"

"Paraffin, my dear," she replied seriously. She turned away from the mirror as she spoke, and came face to face with Joan.

"Hullo!" said Joan, smiling in a friendly way.

"Hello! What a crush! Why don't they have more mirrors? How can anyone see themselves with hundreds of women crawling up their backs!"

Joan had not seen herself at all, but she was not worrying unduly, for she was comfortably aware that her face required few artificial enhancements. The comfortable feeling vanished, however, when she realised that Erica was staring at her nose.

"Is it a smut or something?" she enquired anxiously.

"How d'you get rid of freckles?" demanded Erica.

"I never have them —"

"Nonsense! You had several on your nose the other day . . . I saw them distinctly . . . of course you don't have to tell me how you get rid of them if you don't want to, but you needn't lie about it," declared Erica with alarming frankness.

140

Joan gasped — it is unusual for a complete stranger to call you a liar to your face — she saw how right Jane had been in saying that this girl was dangerous. Not only was she more observant than anybody has a right to be, but she was also more outspoken.

"Oatmeal and milk," murmured Joan. "I can't tell you now."

Erica was appeased, she nodded understandingly. "You leave it on all night, I suppose," she said. "Tell me some other time. I've tried all sorts of things — as a matter of fact I rather like a few unobtrusive freckles in the daytime, but they look frightful at night."

By this time the ladies were moving slowly towards the ballroom, and Joan moved too, squeezed in amongst them like a sardine.

"I thought you knew Miss Fortune, Mrs. Prestcott!" said Erica in significant tones.

"I thought so, too," declared Mrs. Prestcott acidly.

"Oh dear, how silly of me!" Joan exclaimed. "People look so different in evening frocks." She smiled sweetly at Harold's mother as she spoke, but the smile was not returned, and Joan became aware that Harold's mother did not like her — or at least did not like Jane. Mrs. Prestcott was destined to like her even less before the evening was over, but neither of them knew this, of course.

The lounge had been cleared and presented a gay appearance with masses of flowers and strings of coloured lights. The band had started to play "My Boy can Dance" — Joan's favourite tune — and the floor looked smooth and inviting. She felt a surge of excitement sweep over her . . . it was going to be fun . . . it was going to be lovely . . . she was going to enjoy every moment of it.

Harold, who was waiting at the door for his mother, caught the look of rapturous anticipation upon Miss Fortune's face. It made her more beautiful than ever, and also, somehow, more approachable. It was the look of a little girl arriving at a party, "Here I am," it seemed to say. "Here I am all dressed up and ready, who wants to dance with me?" Harold did not hesitate, he darted to her side, and the next moment his arm was round her waist, and they were gliding off together across the empty floor, their steps suited admirably.

"The fair Miss Fortune has stolen Harold. How tiresome for you!" remarked Giles to his sister in the usual amiable manner of the Manleys.

Erica did not reply. She *was* annoyed to see Harold spirited off before her eyes. Harold was her host (for she and Giles were staying the night at Suntrap) and, being her host, he surely owed her a little consideration . . . besides, Harold had belonged to her for some time in his queer doggy way and it was useful to have him at her beck and call.

She was annoyed with Harold, but even more annoyed with Giles for seeing and commenting upon his defection. Giles had better mind his own business (thought Erica) or he would live to regret it. There were various means of getting her own back upon Giles, and Erica knew how to use them.

Mrs. Prestcott was far more angry than Erica when she saw Harold glide off with Miss Fortune, for it was an understood thing that Harold should dance the first dance with his mother — it looked well — and should then find her a comfortable seat, well out of the draught, to which she could lay claim for the remainder of the evening.

As for Colonel Staunton, he was quite livid with rage to see his English Rose appropriated by "that pup Prestcott". Surely the first dance should be dedicated to one's host — it was always so in his young days. He stood at the door and glowered so fiercely that everybody avoided him like the plague.

Miss Ames however who was rather short sighted, but too vain to wear glasses, saw the Colonel's face as a formless blur. She thought he looked lonely with nobody to talk to, so she bore down upon him full of Christian charity, and remarked that it was delightful to see the young people having a good time. Colonel Staunton did not think so at all; he wanted to have a good time himself, not to see others having it, so he muttered something, fortunately unintelligible, and turned away.

Meanwhile Joan was enjoying herself thoroughly; she had promised to "be good", and that meant dancing with Colonel Staunton, who was her host, but the poor Colonel was old and somewhat slow off the mark, and Giles and Harold and Archie Wickham, not to speak of Mr. Green (the Vicar's brother-in-law) were ready and waiting to pounce upon her whenever she was free, and bear her off.

Every time that this occurred Joan murmured feebly, "But I ought to dance with Colonel Staunton —

really." And, every time Giles or Harold, or whoever it might be, replied instantly: "You can dance with him next time. I simply must have this one," and whirled her away.

There was such a crowd of faces, all unknown, that Joan was almost dizzy trying to differentiate between them, and it was not until nearly the end of the fifth dance on the programme that she became aware of a brown face — familiar in some half forgotten way — and a pair of bright blue eyes which seemed to be watching her in a puzzled, wistful manner from the door. Where had she seen that man? Was it in town, perhaps, or —

"Oh Heavens!" said Joan aloud.

"What?" enquired Giles, who was her partner for the moment. "Did I bump you? I'm frightfully sorry."

"No, but I must stop — I must speak to somebody," Joan declared. She had suddenly realised that the brown face and blue eyes belonged to "Charles", the man she had met in Mrs. Trail's shop. Jane had said that he was not coming, but here he was as large as life and twice as natural. She realised also, that he must have been here for ages — perhaps from the very beginning of the dance — and that she, not expecting to see him, had probably cut him dead. It was all the more frightful because Jane liked this Charles quite a lot — Joan was sure of it by the expression on her face when she spoke of him. The situation was truly desperate.

The man with the brown face had turned away, and was disappearing out of the door. Joan tore herself from her partner's arms and pursued him bumping into the still-revolving couples in her haste. He was in the hall, waiting for his coat to be found when Joan burst through the crowd and seized his arm. Even now her troubles were only beginning for she had no idea what to say, nor how to explain her apparently extraordinary behaviour.

"Where are you going? I thought you weren't coming," she babbled nervously.

He did not answer, but stood and looked down at her with a strange, puzzled stare.

"Have you been here long?" she asked, in a frantic endeavour to make him speak to her.

"You saw me," Charles said.

"I didn't — honestly," she declared. "How could I know you were coming when you said you wouldn't be here!"

"I changed my mind. I thought — I thought you might be glad to see me —"

"I am . . . of course I am . . . are you going to dance with me?"

"I only looked in for a minute — I'm going home."

"Don't be angry with me — do stay and dance."

"I can't stay," said Charles firmly.

The whole conversation had lasted but a few moments, it was carried out in low hurried tones. Giles, who had pursued his errant partner, now arrived upon the scene, also the club steward with Charles' coat.

"Hullo, Charles — you're not going away!" exclaimed Giles in amazement.

"Yes, I'm going home," said Charles shortly.

The club steward held out his coat, and he put it on.

"Come tomorrow . . . come and see me," Joan besought him, clutching his arm as he turned away. "Come to tea tomorrow — please do — I'll explain everything."

Charles did not reply. He bowed gravely and turned away.

"The good Charles seems a bit fed up!" remarked Giles, with a laugh.

CHAPTER
EIGHTEEN

The next dance was now starting and Harold was waiting to claim Joan as his partner. She was rather glad to see him for he was a comforting sort of person and she needed consolation badly.

"Don't let's dance," she said.

He agreed at once, for, although it was delightful to dance with Joan, it would be almost better to sit and talk to her. He led her to the refreshment room, which was almost empty, and found two chairs in a corner. It was perfectly clear to Harold that his partner was worried and upset — though he did not know why — and being of a tactful and sensitive nature he fetched her a cup of tea and placed it in her hands. Tea was as balm in Gilead to feminine troubles as Harold was well aware from long experience of his mother.

"Thank you . . . you are a dear," said Joan gratefully.

She sipped her tea and thought about the frightful mess she had made. There was only one thing to be done. Jane must see Charles and explain everything. It was a pity of course, but there was no other way. Joan had ceased to be so terrified of Delaine by this time, for she had been here nearly a week and there were no signs of the man. Perhaps he had forgotten about her by now . . . perhaps she had been a fool to worry . . . he would not bother to come all the way to Dingleford to look for her . . .

Harold saw that the little pucker of distress was disappearing from between his partner's eyes and he congratulated himself upon his foresight in providing her with tea. Now that she was feeling better it was time to talk to her, to entertain her, and take her mind off her troubles — whatever they might be.

He racked his brains for something which would amuse her . . .

"I had such a funny adventure after I had left you yesterday," he said at last and launched forth into an account of the large Frenchman whom he had encountered in Widgett's bar.

The story was quite amusing — as told by Harold — but he had not gone far before he realised that his companion was not amused. On the contrary she was horrified and distressed, her fair face grew quite pale and her grey eyes widened.

"Oh Mr. Prestcott!" she cried, "You didn't tell him I was here, did you?"

"But it wasn't you he was looking for — it was your sister," Harold pointed out.

Joan saw her blunder and saw too, how right she had been to conceal her presence in Dingleford from Dingleford eyes.

"Of course, how silly of me!" she agreed, heaving a sigh of relief to think that she was still safe.

"You don't like him?" Harold asked. It was pretty obvious that she did not like him, of course, but Harold wanted to be sure.

"Like him! I hate him!" cried Joan. "He's a dreadful, horrible man — you don't *know* how horrible he is! I'm terrified of him."

Harold was appalled. Could any man be so utterly base as to alarm and distress Miss Fortune? It was incredible.

"The — the b - beast!" stammered Harold. "If only I had known . . . I'd have . . . I'd have knocked him down or something, instead of standing him a drink. Oh Goodness, I wish I had known!"

Miss Fortune laughed. It certainly *was* ludicrous to think of Harold knocking down the enormous Frenchman, but she was pleased to think he was such a fearless champion all the same.

"I *would* knock him down," Harold cried. "Why, of course I would. Anybody who — who wasn't nice to you —"

"It's *sweet* of you," she declared, smiling at him kindly.

Harold was dazzled by the smile. "I say," he said, "I say, you won't mind if I ask you something, will you . . . d'you think I could call you Jane?"

"Oh . . ." she began, and paused.

"Please let me."

"It's not *that*," explained Miss Fortune, somewhat enigmatically. "It's just . . . well . . . do you think 'Jane' is a nice name?"

"I think it's a *lovely* name," he replied — and indeed he thought, and had thought for days, that it was the most beautiful name on earth.

"Well, I don't," said Miss Fortune. "I mean," she added hastily as she saw his surprise, "I mean 'Jane' is all right in its way, but it doesn't really suit me, somehow. People can't choose their own names, can they?"

"Of course not," he agreed, nodding earnestly, "or I shouldn't be called 'Harold'. I see what you mean, now."

"All my real friends call me 'Joan'," she told him truthfully.

"May I?" cried Harold, his eyes shining with eagerness.

"Yes, if you like," smiled Miss Fortune. "You may call me 'Joan', but it must be a secret, an absolutely dead secret, because other people might think it was silly. You may only call me 'Joan' when we're alone together."

Harold promised to observe this law. He was uplifted to the Seventh Heaven at the mark of confidence from his divinity.

At this moment Mrs. Prestcott swept into the refreshment room on Colonel Staunton's arm. She was in a thoroughly bad temper because she had been sitting for hours in a thorough draught and had had no sustenance of any description. It was only by the grace of God that she had managed to entrap Colonel Staunton and inveigle him into bringing her to the

150

refreshment room for a cup of tea. Harold should hear about it when they got home.

"Tea or lemonade?" enquired the Colonel politely.

"Tea, *please*," replied Mrs. Prestcott, shuddering. Her lips felt quite blue beneath their paint and her back and arms were disfigured by goose flesh. It will be a miracle if I'm not in bed with pleurisy or something, she thought, clenching her teeth to prevent them from chattering like castanets.

She sipped her tea and looked round the room, and suddenly her eyes fell upon the couple in the corner — Harold and that girl! Harold's face was transfigured with heavenly bliss, but the assurance that her son was enjoying himself brought no pleasure to his mother's heart.

"So kind of you to take pity on me," she murmured to Colonel Staunton, with a brave smile. "*So* kind. I thought Miss Fortune was your guest this evening?"

"Er — yes," said the Colonel unhappily.

"Then why don't you dance with her?" enquired Mrs. Prestcott. She almost added "you old fool" but managed to bite back the words in time.

Colonel Staunton was somewhat surprised at the interest Mrs. Prestcott was showing in his affairs — it was deuced good of her, he thought. "I haven't had a chance to —" he began.

"Now's your chance, Colonel, you don't expect her to ask you to dance with her, do you," said his companion playfully.

"Er — no," replied Colonel Staunton. He looked at the couple in the corner doubtfully, for they were so intent upon each other that he could not believe they would welcome interruption.

"I believe you're frightened," declared Mrs. Prestcott.

He laughed. It was absurd to think that he, who had led his men at Ypres, should be frightened to approach a pretty girl.

"Well, it looks like it," Mrs Prestcott pointed out.

"But what about you?" enquired her partner. "I mean you would be all by yourself —"

"You *are* frightened," cried Mrs. Prestcott with an arch look, and she patted him lightly on the arm. "You *are* frightened, Colonel. Come now, I dare you to do it!" She was really desperate.

Colonel Staunton was delighted and amused. "All right," he said. "All right, Mrs. Prestcott, you watch me. I'll show you the kind of stuff that the Old Contemptibles are made of."

He finished his hock-cup at one gulp and bore down upon the couple in the corner with a courageous mien. Joan surrendered without a shot and was borne off to the ballroom in triumph, and Harold was appropriated by his mother who enquired with alarming sweetness as to what he had been doing with himself.

Joan was especially charming to the Colonel to make up for her previous neglect. She danced twice with him and allowed him to take her in to supper as Jane had suggested, then she danced with Archie Wickham and with Mr. Ames. She was still a little worried about Charles, but it was impossible to remain gloomy in view of the attention she was receiving; she was the most

152

sought after girl in the room — not only because she was pretty and charming, but also because she was NEW. The Dingleford residents had known each other for years and were constantly meeting in the village or on the links, so a new face and a new personality were distinctly intriguing.

Harold was tied to his mother until the last dance of the evening, and then escaped from her clutches and made a beeline for Joan. They smiled at each other and glided off.

"I saw you dancing with Ames," Harold said, as he manoeuvred her carefully round the room. "Did he tell you that a bird in the hand is worth two in the bush?"

"No, he said that 'none but the brave deserve the fair'. I think he's *nice*," she added teasingly, "much, much nicer than you, for instance."

This sort of badinage was not in Harold's line, for he was too unsure of himself to enjoy the personal insults which are so popular a form of wit amongst present day youth. He did not answer and looked so dejected and doggy-eyed that the tender hearted Joan relented at once.

"You know I didn't mean it, silly," she told him kindly.

PART THREE

CHAPTER
NINETEEN

When Charles left the club house he was furiously angry, but, before he had found Edgar and got him started, his anger had begun to give place to bewilderment. Charles got into his car and sat there, trying to puzzle it out. How extraordinary Jane's behaviour had been! He had arrived at the dance and had stationed himself at the door of the ballroom, all ready to surprise her with a smile and an explanation of his change of plan. As usual his speech had been carefully thought out: "Got through the London business sooner than I expected," he was going to say, "so I thought I'd come. How many dances may I have?" The smile and speech were ready but were never delivered, for Jane had looked straight through him with a blank stare. Unable to believe his eyes, Charles had hung about the door and had stood in her path twice with deliberate intent — and twice she had looked through him, not exactly rudely, but simply as if she had never seen him in her life. He had often heard other fellows say that girls were fickle and incalculable, but this was beyond everything — there was something more than mere fickleness here.

Then, suddenly, when she was dancing with Giles he had met her eyes and had seen the surprised look of recognition which had dawned in them. He had thought, *she didn't know me before*, and then, immediately jettisoning the absurd idea — *but that is impossible!* It was utterly absurd and impossible that Jane had not recognised him (Charles could not believe it) but he did not know what else to believe. *I must get out of here* was his next thought and he had turned away, pushing through the crowd of people at the door with scant ceremony — and Jane had followed him. Charles had felt the light touch on his arm and had found her standing beside him, smiling, friendly, apologetic — but (here was the queerest thing of all) instead of feeling the surge of gladness at her dearness and nearness which he surely ought to have felt, he had experienced a feeling of strangeness and had realised that the magnetic attraction of Jane had gone. She was divinely pretty, he saw that, but saw it in a completely cold-blooded way . . . *he didn't love her any more!*

Could people fall out of love like this? Charles would not have believed it, but there it was: this girl, who, only a few days ago, had made the sun shine brighter and sent the world spinning round at twice its usual pace, was now merely a pretty girl and nothing more. "I'm ill," said Charles to himself. "There's something the matter with me —"

He manoeuvred Edgar out of the press and drove slowly home.

★　★　★

Emma Weatherby was in bed but not asleep for it was still quite early. She was amazed to hear the car drive into the garage — amazed and somewhat alarmed — so when Charles passed her door on his way to bed she called to him to come in and speak to her.

"Not asleep yet?" he asked, smiling at her in a queer vague sort of way.

"No, it's early," said Emma.

Charles shut the door and came in. He wandered round her room without speaking and looked so gloomy that Emma was quite alarmed. "Did you feel ill?" she enquired anxiously.

"No, just bored," replied Charles. He knew that Emma wanted to hear about the dance, but for once he was in no mood to tell her anything. "Erica was there," he said, trying to spur himself on. "She had rather a pretty green dress on, she looked nice, I thought. Mrs. Prestcott was in grey satin and diamonds —"

"Was Jane Fortune there?"

"Yes."

"How did she look?"

"Oh quite nice. She had a pink dress." He gloomed for a little longer and then asked: "What do you think of Miss Fortune — truthfully?"

Emma scarcely knew how to reply. She thought Jane was adorable, but it was part of her deep laid plan not to enthuse over her to Charles.

"She's very attractive," said Emma.

Charles laughed grimly. "All right, don't worry," he said "I know you can't bear the sight of her and neither can I."

His mother was so startled by this extraordinary statement that she abandoned her scheme forthwith.

"Charles! But I *do* like her. I think she's perfectly sweet."

"You don't," said Charles. "You can't deceive me, Emma Weatherby. I know you can't *stand* the girl and you're right. There's something queer about her . . . she's double-faced."

It was so unlike Charles to speak in this wild way that Emma was dismayed. What could have happened? He had spent days at the cottage, and she had hugged herself in the conviction that Charles was in love with Jane (there were unmistakable signs of it — quite unmistakable) and the more Emma had seen of Jane Fortune the more delighted she had been. This was the very girl for Charles, good all through, kindly, friendly, sensible and as pretty as you could find in a day's march — what more could anyone want? Emma had already, in her own mind, fixed the date for the wedding and decided on her own frock for the occasion and now the whole thing had gone wrong. They had quarrelled, she supposed, though it was extremely unlike Charles to quarrel with anybody.

Can I *do* anything, thought Emma desperately. Could I ask what the trouble is? Shall I interfere and try to put things right or would that only make matters worse?

"I shan't go tomorrow. She asked me, but I shan't go," Charles was saying gloomily. "She can clear up the place herself, or get one of her young men to clear it."

"Young men! Has she got young men?" enquired Emma in surprise.

"Dozens!" declared Charles with conviction.

Emma sighed, this was more serious than she had thought. "Jane doesn't look that kind of girl to me," she told him.

"I don't know what kind of girl she is," said Charles wretchedly.

Emma said no more.

During the following twenty-four hours Charles changed his mind about twelve times: he wouldn't go, not he. Why should he bother? He hadn't *said he* would go, so there was no need to do anything more about it . . . or should he go and demand an explanation? Perhaps that would be the best plan, for he could then put the whole thing out of his mind . . . No, he wouldn't do that either, he would go and be quite pleasant to Jane Fortune . . . pleasant but cold, that was more dignified . . . But then, wouldn't it be more dignified not to go at all? Yes, let her make the first move. Let her come to him — if she wanted to come — and explain — if explanation were possible.

Emma watched him anxiously, she was convinced that Charles would make himself ill. He mooched about the house; he mooched about the garden; he sat down and read — without turning over a single page; he let his pipe go out and sat with it clenched between his teeth.

At three o'clock Charles decided definitely that he was not going to tea with Jane Fortune, but by 3.15 he was out in the garage, fiddling with Edgar's plugs.

"This is ridiculous," said Charles aloud. "I've said I'm not going, and I'm not."

He slid into the driving-seat and sat there thinking. "Look here!" he said firmly, "If Edgar starts the first time I shove in the self-starter I'll go; that's fair."

It was not altogether fair, really, for Edgar had never been known to start at the first shove. Even if he were in one of his better moods it took three good shoves before he showed any signs of life.

Charles pushed in the self-starter and Edgar started immediately. It was Fate . . . or perhaps it was merely because the engine was warm and the plugs newly cleaned. Whatever it was Charles was now bound to go to tea with Jane Fortune. He crashed in his gears and moved off.

Emma heard him go.

CHAPTER
TWENTY

Charles found Miss Fortune sitting in the parlour drinking tea. She looked somewhat pale, and there were dark shadows under her eyes, but her smile was as gay and friendly as ever.

"Hullo, Charles — how nice of you to come!" she exclaimed.

He took her outstretched hand, and, quite suddenly, he was in love again . . . the whole world rocked. "Jane!" he cried, "Jane . . . I say . . . I say, Jane . . ."

Nannie, after ushering him in, had shut the door and gone. She was very fond of Charles — he was almost like one of the family — and if Miss Jane wanted to have tea alone with the 'Capting' why shouldn't she? Nannie did not even listen at the door, she went right away and left them to it.

"Come and sit down," said Miss Fortune, drawing her hand away.

Charles sat down and gazed at her. She was sweet; she was simply adorable. What on earth had been the matter with him?

"I can't understand it," said Charles.

"What can't you understand?"

"You . . . me," he replied. "I mean you haven't been the same . . . or else I haven't —"

It was a most extraordinary statement but Miss Fortune seemed to understand. It even seemed as though she were pleased about it, for a little secret smile curved her mouth, and her eyes dwelt upon her visitor in a more-than-friendly way.

"Have you noticed a difference in me?" she enquired. "Really and truly? Was I nicer, or not so nice?"

"Not nearly so nice," declared Charles promptly. "You weren't you at all . . . if you see what I mean . . . I mean . . . well, I don't know what I mean . . ."

"I haven't been feeling quite myself," she told him truthfully.

"You didn't seem *ill*," continued Charles, "but just . . . sort of . . . different."

Jane nodded understandingly. "I've been worried," she said, still speaking nothing but the truth, for indeed she had been worried, lying in bed sneezing, and her double ranging round Dingleford in her skin. She knew full well that there was an imp of mischief in Joan. You could never be quite certain what she would do or say.

"I'm better now," continued Jane frankly. "I'm myself again. Don't let's talk about it any more — unless you want to, of course."

Here was the opening for which Charles had hoped. He could ask her anything he liked; he could ask for a full explanation of her extraordinary behaviour at the dance, but somehow or other it did not matter now, for the dance was past and gone, and past and gone were all his doubts and fears. Jane was Jane again, as perfect and adorable as ever.

"No," said Charles. "Don't let's talk about it any more."

It was obviously the right answer, for Jane leant forward and patted his knee.

"Let's talk about you," she said. "Did you enjoy your visit to London? What did you do?"

"I thought about you," Charles told her. "I thought about you all the time. Jane, do you like me at all?"

"I like you quite a lot," she replied, smiling at him. "Oh Charles, how silly you are! How could anyone help liking you?"

Charles was about to take advantage of this promising opening when the door was flung open and Harold Prestcott walked in. Charles and Jane sprang apart, and faced the newcomer, who advanced upon them with a beaming smile, Francesca at his heels. He was a little disappointed to find Charles having tea with Miss Fortune for Charles' presence would prevent him from calling her 'Joan'. However he would call her Jane, and they would both enjoy the joke.

"I thought I'd drop in and see how you were feeling after the dance, *Jane*," he said, looking at her with a significant twinkle in his eyes.

Jane said it was very nice of him, but she said it coldly. She had thought Mr. Prestcott shy, but apparently he was nothing of the kind. She had no idea of the encouragement he had received during the last few days, of course.

"I've mended the bell again," he continued. "Nannie asked me to. It doesn't take a minute if you know how."

"That's very kind," declared Miss Fortune in warmer tones. "Very kind indeed. Come and have some tea."

In spite of the warmer tone there was something strange to Harold in Miss Fortune's manner, she was different today, but perhaps that was because of Charles. He decided to wait until Charles had gone and then they would have one of their nice cosy talks together.

Unfortunately Charles had the same idea, the idea that he would sit Harold out, for it was absolutely essential to know just exactly what Jane had meant when she said she liked him. How much did she like him and in what way?

Francesca, who remembered her previous insults in this room, had lingered by the door looking somewhat sulky.

"Is that your pug?" enquired Miss Fortune sweetly. "What a darling!"

"It's Francesca!" Harold said, looking at her in amazement. "You don't like dogs —"

"Of course I like them," cried Jane indignantly. "I'm thinking of getting one myself. Come here, Francesca, would you like a piece of cake?"

Harold was stricken dumb. He watched Francesca being stroked and fed with chocolate cake, and decided that girls were the strangest creatures on God's earth. Only two days ago Miss Fortune had declared with vehemence that she did not like dogs (and Harold had not blamed her, for he was thoroughly bored with

166

Francesca himself.) And now she said she *did* like dogs, and was feeding Francesca on the fat of the land. It was small matter perhaps whether or not Miss Fortune was a canophilist but Harold had always been of the opinion that a love of dogs was a fundamental sort of thing; you either liked them immensely all your life, or else you found them utterly revolting. Harold could find no possible explanation for Miss Fortune's change of tune. There was nothing to be *said*, of course, even if he had not been stricken dumb with astonishment, for it would have puzzled a diplomat to have worded a tactful enquiry on the subject. Without inferring that Miss Fortune was a liar Harold could do nothing to solve the mystery, so the mystery must remain unsolved.

Sated with cake, Francesca lay down and snored — it was one of her least endearing habits — and the three human beings were at liberty to get on with their tea, and their conversation.

They sat and talked about all manner of things, about the dance (this was Harold's subject) and about the fire, and about the European Situation and eventually about the weather. The atmosphere grew more and more strained and at last the visitors saw that the thing was hopeless. They gave in and rose at the same moment.

"Come along Harold, we'll walk home together," Charles said, for, if he were to have no further conversation with Jane himself, he would see to it that Harold had none either.

Harold hesitated. He had decided to go, of course, but if Charles were going perhaps he might remain for another ten minutes — ten minutes was better than nothing.

"That *will* be nice for you," said Jane firmly. "It's such a long dreary road, isn't it?"

They left together, with Francesca of course, and Jane saw them off at the door.

CHAPTER
TWENTY-ONE

Now that they were alone, and there was no woman to disturb their minds, Charles and Harold became more friendly. They did not talk much as they walked along for they were both somewhat exhausted by the silent battle which had been waged in Miss Fortune's parlour. They walked up the long road to the village and as they passed the Cat and Fiddle their pace slowed down.

"Come in and have a drink," Charles suggested. He had a vague feeling that Emma had said something about giving Harold a drink. Her actual words were obliterated by all that had happened, but the feeling that Emma wanted him to give Harold a drink remained.

Widgett was smiling and welcoming as usual, he drew two pints and set them before his visitors without a word, and without a word, the two glasses were emptied.

"Ah, I needed that!" said Charles.

"I saw you did," declared Widgett, beaming. "Ho yes, you gets to know people's moods! I jes ses to myself when I sees you walk in, 'these two young gents wants a drink badly,' I ses," he laughed.

Charles and Harold laughed too, at first a bit creakily, but afterwards with more gusto, for Widgett's good-nature was infectious.

The only other occupant of the bar was an old man with a fringe of white whisker round his apple-cheeked face; he was sitting at a small table in the corner and was watching the young gentlemen with bright beady eyes.

Charles and Widgett discussed racing, and the chances of an outsider winning tomorrow's three thirty. Widgett had got a tip which he declared was "straight from the 'orse's mouth." It was "Fair Beauty" at 20 to 1. Harold listened with interest to the account of this animal's parentage, speed and staying power. He had never had a bet in his life, but, as Mr. Ames would have said, one was "never too old to learn" and his mother need never know a thing about it. "What the eye does not see —" thought Harold, (this was another of Mr. Ames' favourite sayings.)

"How do you *do* it?" enquired Harold, interrupting the conversation in his eagerness to learn.

" 'Ow d'you do what?" asked Widgett.

"How do you put money on a horse?"

" 'Ow do you — are you 'avin' me on?"

"No, I want to know how you do it."

"You does it with a bookie of course," declared Widgett, scarcely able to believe his ears.

"Yes, but how? I mean how do you *find* a bookie?"

"That's good, that is — 'ow d'you find a bookie — that's rich."

"I want to put some money on Fair Beauty, you see," Harold explained. Fair Beauty, he thought, what a name! Of course Fair Beauty would win — it was bound to.

"I'll do it for you if you like," said Widgett promptly.

Harold immediately took out his note case and laid two ten pound notes on the counter.

"What! A pony!" cried Widgett amazed.

"I thought it was a horse —" began Harold in bewildered tones.

"It *is* a norse," said Widgett patiently, "Fair Beauty at 20 to 1, that's wot it is."

"But then you said it was a pony."

"It *is* a pony . . . wot I means is," said Widgett, getting more and more muddled, "Wot I means is you wants to put a pony on a norse —"

Harold saw it now, for he was a quick learner. His face brightened. "Yes," he said. "Yes, can you do it for me?"

"I can *do* it, all right."

"Well, take it then," said Harold, pushing the money towards him.

Widgett gathered up the notes tenderly and then he hesitated and looked at Charles: "Does 'e *know?*" enquired Widgett in a low voice.

Charles was shaking with laughter, but he controlled himself and explained to Harold that if the horse did not win he would lose his money.

"Of course," replied Harold, "I'm not such a fool as that; but the horse *will* win, you'll see, and the more I put on it the more I shall get back. Twenty times twenty is four hundred — what a good thing I happened to go to the bank this afternoon!"

It was obvious that Harold was in full possession of his wits; in fact his words carried so much conviction that afterwards, when Widgett rang up his own particular bookie to make Harold's bet, he trebled his own stake on Fair Beauty. There was something in young Mr. Prestcott's eye, Widgett thought, something a bit fey — and beginner's luck was proverbial.

Charles and Harold were embarking upon their second pints when the door swung open and a tall broad figure walked into the bar. Widgett recognised him at once, and so did Harold; but whereas Widgett was quite pleased to see "the foreigner" again, Harold was not.

M. Delaine advanced upon them beaming, quite oblivious of Harold's frown. "Ha, my ole frien'," he cried. "We meet again, chin chin! I come from London to 'ave annuzzer look for zat girl I tell you about ze uzzer day."

"Oh, you do, do you?" said Harold fiercely. "Well you can just go back to London then. She doesn't like your ugly face, and neither do I."

"*Comment!*" cried the man, in amazement.

Harold forgot his shyness and repeated his remarks, with variation and additions, in the man's own tongue. The loose translation was even less polite than the original, for if French is a language in which it is possible to be delicately courteous, it is also a language in which one may be gorgeously rude.

172

For a moment M. Delaine was too astonished to reply, but his astonishment soon gave way to wrath and he approached Harold menacingly, his chin advanced, his dark eyes glaring, a stream of gutter French pouring from his lips. Harold was ready for him, he waited until the ugly face was quite near, and then hit out with all his force —

It was a shrewd blow, for a week of exercises had worked wonders, and it was also a lucky one, for it caught Delaine just below the point of the chin. He went over backwards like a felled ox and lay stretched out upon the sanded floor. Harold, not contented with his downfall, leapt upon him in a fine frenzy of rage and prepared to finish him off. He saw no reason to spare a fallen foe, not having had the advantage of a Public School education.

The whole thing had happened so suddenly and unexpectedly that Charles and Widgett were dumbfounded. They were glued to the floor, but seeing Harold still bent upon the utter destruction of his victim, Charles sprang forward and caught his friend by the arm.

"Harold!" he cried, "You can't hit a man when he's down."

"No, but I can kick him!" cried Harold, suiting the action to the word.

By this time Widgett had come to his senses, he leapt over the counter with an agility surprising in a man of his weight and seized Harold's other arm.

" 'Ere, what's 'e done?" cried Widgett. " 'Ere Mr. Prestcott sir, you don't want ter kill 'im."

"I do, I do!" declared Harold, struggling furiously.

"Not in my bar, you won't," said Widgett firmly.

The old man in the corner was chuckling to himself in high glee; it was seldom that such excitement broke the even tenor of Dingleford life.

" 'Urray! 'urray!" he cried in a high squeaky voice. "Let the young gent 'ave another go at 'im, Mister Widgett, do".

Delaine was recovering now; he opened his eyes and saw Harold struggling with his captors. It was not a reassuring sight.

" 'Old 'im tight!" he cried. " 'Old 'im tight! 'E is mad, zat man. *Mad*, I tell you," and with incredible rapidity he scrambled to his feet and staggered out of the door, banging it behind him. They heard his car starting and the spatter of gravel beneath its wheels as he sped away.

Charles and Widgett now released Harold and Widgett produced a large red bandana handkerchief and mopped his brow.

"Well now!" he said. "Well there now, I 'aint seen such a thing for years. Blest if I knows wot it was all about either. Whooph!"

"What a devil you are!" said Charles, half laughingly and half admiringly. "A proper knock-out, wasn't it Widgett?"

"Pretty," agreed Widgett nodding solemnly. "Neat and pretty, I calls it. 'E won't come back for more."

"But what had the fellow *done*, Harold?" Charles enquired. "I mean did you just take a sudden dislike to his face —"

174

"I had my reasons," said Harold primly. He shook himself, settled his tie at Widgett's mirror and smoothed his hair which had become somewhat ruffled in the excitement. He was pleased with himself and justifiably so, for he had done exactly what he had said he would do, and had given the fellow exactly what he deserved — had given it neatly and without unnecessary fuss. The man, as Widgett had observed, would not come back for more; so much the better.

Harold realised that he had been rather lucky to light upon such a vulnerable spot for his blow. Delaine was so much larger than himself that he might have been victorious had the engagement been prolonged, but Harold's cause was just, so the luck had been deserved. Even so had David triumphed over the champion of the Philistines.

" 'E's gorn without drinkin' 'is beer," Widgett said, pointing to the glass on the counter, "an' without payin' for it too . . . but no matter —"

"I'll pay," said Harold. He was feeling nine feet high and as generous as be damned.

"You won't then, sir," declared Widgett smiling. "It was worth a pint o' the best to see you lay out that Frenchy. Ha, ha, it was worth a good bit more! Come along both of you, an' 'ave a drink on the 'ouse. What'll you 'ave? Great it was . . . ha, ha . . . weren't it great, Capting? I know I wouldn't 'ave missed it for a good deal."

Charles agreed enthusiastically.

CHAPTER
TWENTY-TWO

We must now return to Dingleford Cottage, where Jane Fortune, having despatched her visitors successfully, returned to the parlour and lay down on the sofa to rest. She was very tired, for she had only just arisen from a bed of sickness, and although her illness had been neither serious nor prolonged, it had lowered her vitality considerably. The tea-party, at which she had played the part of hostess had been a most trying affair, enough to tire a person of robust health, let alone a convalescent, for the atmosphere had been so strained and uncomfortable that it had taken all her diplomacy to avert a storm. Jane smiled to herself as she snuggled down amongst the cushions. How angry Charles had been at the interruption to their cosy *tête à tête!* He looked as if he could have slain Mr. Prestcott then and there. And Mr. Prestcott had been almost as difficult as Charles, from a hostess's point of view. He had insisted upon discussing the dance, a subject which Jane was particularly anxious to avoid, and he had kept on smiling and nodding at her whenever he mentioned her name, as if there were some joke about it. Charles had not liked that, and had grown more and more grumpy and bearish every moment.

In a way it was rather nice that Charles had resented Harold Prestcott's behaviour, and Jane would not have minded if the sitting had not lasted so long, but when time went on and on and neither of her visitors had shown any signs of departing, she had begun to wish them both at the bottom of the sea. Men *are* troublesome, thought Jane. However they had gone now, thank goodness and peace was restored in her cosy little parlour. Peace and silence, how lovely they were. Jane did not even want Joan to talk to, she just wanted to be alone. I'm too tired, she thought sleepily, too tired to talk to anybody . . . much . . . too . . . tired.

Jane was almost, if not quite asleep, when the parlour door was flung open and Mrs. Prestcott was announced; the last person that Jane expected to see. She sprang up from the sofa conscious of a flushed face and tousled hair, but there was no time to titivate. Mrs. Prestcott sailed in with a swish of silken garments, looking as if she had stepped out of a fashion plate. She was wearing a green and white patterned foulard trimmed with pleated frills and a large black hat with a green flower in it.

Jane was surprised that Mrs. Prestcott should call because the last time that lady had called at the cottage she had left in a precipitate manner, furious at the destruction of the shrubbery which she had cherished so assiduously and for so long. Jane had formed the opinion that Mrs. Prestcott would return no more to Dingleford Cottage and had had no cause to change it. Perhaps I'm asleep and dreaming, thought Jane and she pinched herself to see if the vision would vanish, for she had read somewhere that this was the right procedure to prove oneself awake. Far from vanishing, however, Mrs. Prestcott's image became more real and Jane was forced to the reluctant conclusion that it was not a dream.

"How d'you do, Mrs. Prestcott?" enquired Jane in the conventional manner and she smiled as cordially as she could for although she did not care for Mrs. Prestcott, she had no wish to be inhospitable. "How nice of you to come!" she added. "I'll ring for sherry, shall I? Or would you rather have a cup of tea?"

Mrs. Prestcott ignored Jane's outstretched hand. She bowed formally and declared that she had had tea and did not want sherry.

"Come and sit down then," said Jane, somewhat puzzled by her strange behaviour.

Mrs. Prestcott sat down on the sofa, spreading out her dress so that the sofa was completely occupied. Jane sat down opposite to her in a chair.

"First of all I wish to apologise for calling upon you at this late hour," said Mrs. Prestcott in a cold level voice. "I was obliged to hire a car to bring me here and this was the only time the car was available. There is only one car for hire in the whole of Dingleford apparently."

"Yes, I know," said Jane. "It belongs to Mrs. Trail's son, doesn't it? What a frightful bore for you, but I thought you had a car of your own."

"I have a car, but I don't drive it myself, and, as I have no chauffeur, I am dependant upon — but that is no concern of yours."

"I am very glad to see you," Jane declared with more politeness than truth. "I suppose you have come —" and then she stopped. She had supposed that Mrs. Prestcott had come to fetch her son, but somehow or other she was suddenly aware that this was not so, and that Mrs. Prestcott did not know that her son had been at Dingleford Cottage to tea and had better not be told.

Mrs. Prestcott smiled in a far from pleasant manner. "I see that you have realised the reason for my visit so there is no need for me to tell you. Please do not say that you are 'glad to see me', Miss Fortune, there is nothing to be gained by beating about the bush."

"I don't know what you mean!" cried Jane in amazement.

"You know what I mean perfectly well," declared her visitor.

"No," said Jane, shaking her head.

"I was quite ready to be friendly," continued Mrs. Prestcott plaintively. "I was willing to help you in every way I could, but your behaviour has been so — so extraordinary that unless you mend your ways I can have nothing more to do with you."

Jane was annoyed and replied with some heat: "It's *your* behaviour that's extraordinary, not mine. Dingleford Cottage belongs to me now and I can do what I like. Why should I ask your permission, or anybody's permission, before cutting down a shrubbery on my own ground?" And then, because she had no desire to quarrel with Mrs. Prestcott, she leant forward and smiled. "Don't be vexed about it," she said persuasively. "Look how this room is improved. You like sunshine too, don't you?"

"You needn't try your wiles on me," said Mrs. Prestcott acidly. "I am not to be deceived nor cajoled. You know perfectly well that I have not come here to talk to you about the rhododendron bushes which you have seen fit to destroy, that is your own business and affects nobody but yourself. I have come here to complain of your behaviour. I was horrified at the way you behaved last night at the dance, frankly horrified. I am neither old-fashioned nor narrow-minded but I confess I was shocked."

Jane listened to this tirade with astonishment and growing rage. She was all the more angry because it was Joan who was being accused of unseemly behaviour. Jane might sometimes criticize Joan herself, but nobody else in the world had any right to say a word against her. Besides, thought Jane, it's all *lies*. Joan wouldn't do anything horrid, this woman is crazy. Jane was so angry and upset that for a moment she was speechless.

Mrs. Prestcott misread her silence and thought that the battle was won. Mrs. Prestcott had found that bullying paid, for few people had the courage to stand up to her. She could cow the wretched Harold with a few harsh words and she saw no reason why the same treatment should not succeed with Jane Fortune.

She smoothed out her dress — it was really armour, of course, and she had taken a good deal of trouble over her *toilette de guerre* — and continued sternly, "If you will apologise and agree to mend your ways I shall say no more about it. You have no mother and therefore you cannot be blamed. It is ignorance, I suppose. That is why I came here today to reason with you. You see, Miss Fortune, I was sorry for you when you came here first, and I did all I could for you. I actually asked my friends to call on you, so of course I feel responsible for your behaviour."

Jane found her voice. "How kind of you!" she observed in a far from grateful tone.

"My intentions *were* kind," declared Mrs. Prestcott, who resented the satire and was losing her temper rapidly. "My intentions were kind whether you believe it or not, but my feelings have undergone a change. I saw last night what sort of person you were and I wish to have nothing more to do with you."

"This is extraordinary!" cried Jane, her eyes flashing fire. "This is unbearable! Do you mean that you hired a car and came down here to tell me this — that you didn't want to have anything more to do with me? Surely it would have been easier, if that's how you feel, to ignore me altogether. I haven't troubled you much, have I? I haven't been inside your house since I came to live at Dingleford. That doesn't look as if I wanted your patronage, does it?"

Mrs. Prestcott went pale with fury. "You know perfectly well why I came," she cried. "I intended to spare you the shame of hearing the truth, but you are shameless. If your behaviour at the dance had been merely thoughtless and foolish I could have overlooked it because you are young and have no mother —"

181

"Please leave my mother out of it!" Jane exclaimed.

"But you were worse than foolish, you were wicked. You know quite well that I am referring to the way you behaved with my son."

"With your son!"

"You needn't pretend to be surprised . . . everyone in the room was talking about it . . . about the shameless way you threw yourself at his head."

Jane saw the whole thing now and the flame of her rage steadied down. She was still furious with the woman, of course, but her sense of humour was beginning to function and she realised how intensely funny the situation was. Mrs. Prestcott had put herself to considerable trouble and expense to rescue her son from a designing young woman, but all the trouble and expense was wasted because she had got hold of quite the wrong young woman to reason with. Jane saw the humour of it, but she also saw that she must walk very warily. She was entirely in the dark for she had no idea what Joan had done to rouse Mrs. Prestcott's ire nor what her intentions were with regard to the future. She could not believe that Joan was really in love with Harold Prestcott — he was not the type that Jane admired — but it was quite possible that Harold Prestcott was in love with Joan.

Mrs. Prestcott had been watching her face. "Well?" she enquired. "Well, what have you to say for yourself?"

"What does your son say about it?" asked Jane.

This was rather a difficult question to answer, and Mrs. Prestcott hesitated for a moment or two. "I haven't spoken to my son," she said at last. "It is the woman who is to blame in these cases, for the woman always sets the pace. It is *your* behaviour I am complaining about, not his. My son is devoted to me, of course, and I have only to make my wishes known to him . . . he would do anything for me."

"How lucky you are!"

"Your satire does not affect me," declared Mrs. Prestcott angrily. "I know I am lucky in my son. He and I have always been everything to each other. He has never been away from me . . . you couldn't understand of course."

"I shouldn't want to," said Jane with spirit. "If I ever have a son I shall see that he stands on his own feet."

Mrs. Prestcott could not reply to that. She changed her tune a little, for there was still something that she wanted to say to Jane Fortune, something that *must* be said before she could take her departure. "I came here today to speak to you for your own good," said Mrs. Prestcott severely, "and because I dislike seeing a member of my sex make a fool of herself."

Jane laughed; she couldn't help it. "So do I, Mrs. Prestcott," she declared.

"Impertinent . . . brazen and impertinent! Let me tell you that you are doing yourself no good by taking up this attitude, for I am more than ever determined to have nothing to do with you."

"I can't say I'm very sorry," replied Jane.

"Oh, you are unbearable!" cried the outraged lady, rising from the sofa with a rustle of silken frills. "You are simply unbearable! You are never to speak to Harold again, do you hear me?"

"I hear you," said Jane, rising too. "I can promise you faithfully that I shall never speak to your son again unless he speaks to me. You're quite satisfied with that, I suppose, because of course he will do anything you tell him."

Mrs. Prestcott was by no means satisfied, for she did not intend to say a word to Harold — she had that much sense — she glared at Jane in a furious manner, but Jane stared back quite undaunted. She had sized up Mrs. Prestcott pretty accurately and was not in the least frightened of her.

"I suppose you think he will *marry* you," said Mrs. Prestcott scornfully, "but I can tell you quite definitely that he has no intention of doing so. He would never marry anyone that I didn't approve of. You had better leave my son alone, Miss Fortune, for I should never allow it — *never*. You are simply wasting your time pursuing my son."

"Why are you worrying, then, Mrs. Prestcott?" enquired Jane with composure,

Mrs. Prestcott could find no reply whatever to this natural question — perhaps there was none to be found. She turned away in a fury and made for the door and Jane opened it and showed her out. They parted on the doorstep of Dingleford Cottage without the benedictions which are usually exchanged by a hostess and her departing guest for each hoped that she would never see the other again.

CHAPTER
TWENTY-THREE

News travels fast in Dingleford and, like a snowball, increases in size as it rolls on. The old man with the white whiskers, who had been such an interested spectator of the fracas in Widgett's bar, hobbled home as fast as he could and told his wife all about it. She immediately seized her bonnet and ran round the corner to her married daughter and while they were still discussing the affair the postman called with a registered letter. His Majesty's mails were considerably delayed, for the tale of the Homeric battle had to be unfolded to Mr. Fawkes. It was a splendid story by this time. Mr. Fawkes listened to it open-mouthed and went on his way rejoicing and spread it far and wide.

When Mr. Fawkes returned to the post office it was very late, but before sorting the letters with Mrs. Trail, a task that they both enjoyed, he proceeded to inform her of the distorted facts.

"You'd never think," said Mr. Fawkes, leaning over the counter and speaking in confidential tones, "you'd never think that there young Mr. Prestcott was a fire-heater, would you, Mrs. Trail?"

"No, that I shouldn't, an' what's more 'e ain't no such thing," declared Mrs. Trail flatly. "A nice quiet well-mannered young gentleman, that's what 'e is."

Mr. Fawkes laughed excitedly. "That's what *you* think, but you're wrong, see! 'E 'ad a norful set-to this afternoon in Widgett's. It was a foreigner, a girt big ugly lookin' customer . . . they fought like tigers . . . lasted twenty minutes, an' the 'ole place was wrecked."

"You're 'avin' me on!"

"There was ten pounds damage done if there was a penny," continued Mr. Fawkes with gusto. "An' Mr. Widgett got a black eye tryin' to separate 'em. Mr. Prestcott was like a madman, 'e chases the man round an' round landin' 'im the most terrible blows an' 'im shriekin' an' yellin' . . . an' the tables upset, an' glasses smashed, an' the 'ole floor swimmin' in beer. 'I'll kill you!' shouts Mr. Prestcott, an' at last 'e seizes the chap an' pitches 'im over 'is shoulder like a bag of coal."

"Lor'!" exclaimed Mrs. Trail.

"They 'ad to send to 'orbury for a n'ambulance," continued Mr. Fawkes. "A n'ambulance an' a stretcher with two men to carry 'im out . . . not expected to recover, they say."

"Lor'!" exclaimed Mrs. Trail again. "Oh Lor' . . . it's them books."

"Books? What books?"

"Books on exercises I sold 'im. Oh Lor', I wish I'd never seen them books, dangerous, that's what they are. They nearly killed me, they did, an' now this. Oh Lor'!"

Mr. Fawkes was much intrigued by the new light upon the affair and was not satisfied until he had obtained a full account of the transaction which had taken place between Mrs. Trail and young Mr. Prestcott. Mrs. Trail was ready to oblige and described in detail how Mr. Prestcott had come in and what he had said to her, and what she had said to him, how she had thought at first that it was a murder story he wanted, and how he undeceived her. "An' a murder story is what 'e should 'ave 'ad," declared Mrs. Trail, "for murder stories is 'ealthy readin' for young gentlemen — it takes their minds off — but them exercise books . . . well there . . . well . . ."

" 'Ave you got any left?" enquired Mr. Fawkes eagerly.

Mrs. Trail had quite a pile of copies left, she produced them and they were examined with awe. It was felt by both parties that books which could turn a quiet, nervous, and somewhat downtrodden young gentleman into an assaulter and vanquisher of large foreigners in a well conducted bar must possess almost magical powers.

"I'll burn them," declared Mrs. Trail, who felt that the magic contained between the paper covers must be of the black variety. "Yes, I'll burn the lot, that's what I'll do," and she gathered them up off the counter as she spoke.

"No, no, don't you do that," cried Mr. Fawkes in alarm. "Don't you do that, Mrs. Trail. Look at the loss it would be! I'll — I'll buy some of them books myself."

"What? You'll buy some? Not if I knows it."

"Why not?"

"What d'you want with exercise books? You gets plenty of exercising —"

"I'll 'ave a couple all the same," said the postman, somewhat shamefacedly. "They might 'elp me, you see. I got to be strong for my work, 'aven't I?"

"You be strong enough," declared Mrs. Trail.

But, just as no woman is beautiful enough to dispense entirely with aids to beauty, no man is ever strong enough to disdain aids to strength and Mr. Fawkes was determined to possess two of these books. Mrs. Trail, on the other hand, was determined that he should not have them, for she envisaged the frightful trouble and anxiety which she would suffer if Mr. Fawkes should be affected by them in the same manner as young Mr. Prestcott. It was bad enough in all conscience for young gentlemen to lose their sanity and attack strangers unprovoked, but it would be infinitely worse if civil servants started behaving like mad dogs. What would happen to the mails?

"Come on now," said Mr. Fawkes persuasively. "I'll pay for them. 'Ere you are. You don't want to go an' burn them books when you can get good money for them, Mrs. Trail."

Mrs. Trail made no reply, but gathered up the pile of books, pressing them to her ample bosom as fiercely as if they had been her child in danger of ravishment.

Mr. Fawkes saw her determination and grew desperate, he seized a handful of books and tried to tear them from her grasp. They struggled for a moment and then the whole pile fell onto the floor, scattering far and wide like the leaves of an ash tree in a November gale.

"I'll take these," cried Mr. Fawkes, falling to his knees and gathering up the spoil.

188

"No!" cried Mrs. Trail. "No you don't . . . you don't 'ave one of the . . . not if I knows it," and with a great creaking of joints she knelt down like an elephant and clawed at the books.

The shop was really shut of course — only the post office was open — but such niceties of convention were not strictly observed in Dingleford, so there was nothing very extraordinary in the fact that Colonel Staunton, suddenly finding himself short of tobacco, should open the door and walk in. The only light was over the post office counter, and the remainder of the large room was dim and shadowy. Colonel Staunton could see nobody in the shop, but, as the door was not locked and the light was on, he decided that Mrs. Trail could not be far away. He began his speech, couched in propitiatory terms, for he hoped to persuade the law-abiding Mrs. Trail to commit a felony by selling him an ounce of tobacco after hours.

"Are you there, Mrs. Trail?" said Colonel Staunton, peering into the shadows where boots and hams and garden implements and children's undergarments rioted together in unseemly propinquity. "I wonder if you would be so kind . . . I have just made the discovery that my tobacco jar —" He stopped and started back. Two dark forms had suddenly come into view, scrabbling about on the floor. He thought for a moment that they were dogs fighting, but no, they were too large for dogs. Bears fighting, then . . .

One of the dark forms rose slowly onto its hind legs, and this so alarmed the Colonel that he backed towards the door. His hand was on the latch and in another moment he would have gone when Mrs. Trail spoke.

"Yes sir," she said breathlessly. "Tobacco was it, yes sir".

"What on earth were you doing?" enquired the Colonel. He was extremely angry to find that he had been frightened without cause, so angry that he forgot his empty tobacco jar and the necessity to sue humbly for its replenishment. "What the devil d'you mean by . . . by alarming people like that? And you," he added, turning upon the postman who had risen with more agility and was trying to edge his way to the door with his ill-gotten gains. "And you, Fawkes, are you mad or drunk? What have you got behind your back?"

"Books, sir, just a couple of books I was buyin' from Mrs. Trail, that's all, sir."

"Take them away from 'im, sir," implored Mrs. Trail. " 'E's not to 'ave them, they're dangerous, 'orrible things —"

"Dangerous!" exclaimed Colonel Staunton in surprise.

"Yes sir. Ungodly books they be, an' not fit for 'uman beings. Tell 'im 'e's to give them back, tell 'im that."

Colonel Staunton was not unnaturally intrigued. He took the books from the postman's reluctant hands and proceeded to examine them beneath the light which burned over the post-office counter, turning over the pages and looking carefully at the diagrams in the hope of finding something which might justify the adjectives applied to them by Mrs. Trail. The other two occupants of the shop watched him in silence, waiting patiently for his verdict to be pronounced. It was a strange scene, if

190

anybody except the actors had been there to appreciate it; the shop, with its jumble of incongruous objects, half hidden in gloom; Mrs. Trail, fat and worried; Mr. Fawkes anxious but respectful; the Colonel intent upon his task with the light shining down upon his sparse tufty white hair.

"They seem quite — er — harmless," said the Colonel, at last in disappointed tones.

"Dangerous," declared Mrs. Trail firmly. "Dangerous is what they be. Nearly killed me, they did an' now they've done worse. A man's been killed in Mr. Widgett's bar. A 'uman life lost, an' all through them books, sir. An' young Mr. Prestcott 'ad up for murder, an' 'is pore mother's 'eart broken —"

Colonel Staunton was appalled. "What!" he exclaimed. "A man killed! Mr. Prestcott had up for murder!"

"Yes, sir," said Mrs. Trail. "Yes sir, that's what. You see 'ow dangerous them books are."

"Fawkes, is this true?"

"Well sir, in a manner of speaking it's true."

"A thing is either true, or else it isn't true," said Colonel Staunton promptly. "I must get to the bottom of it, Fawkes," and he proceeded to institute enquiries on the orderly room principle and soon had a complete account of the affair. Fawkes who had served in the army during the war was obliged to tone down the story considerably, for he was somewhat in awe of Colonel Staunton and dared not embroider his canvas.

"Did you see the fight with your own eyes?" enquired the Colonel in a booming voice.

"No sir, it was old Doubleday as saw it."

"Did Doubleday tell you about it?"

"No sir, it was Mrs. Doubleday what told me."

"Third hand," declared the Colonel. "Third hand, and you're all liars, every one of you. But still there must be something in it of course. No smoke without fire, as Ames would say."

"No sir," agreed Mr. Fawkes meekly.

"Prestcott probably trounced the man — we can't get away from that — but I've no doubt that the man deserved it."

"Yes sir," agreed Mr. Fawkes.

The colonel's opinion of Harold Prestcott had risen considerably, for he admired a man of spirit as only a man of spirit could. "The young devil," said Colonel Staunton, smiling to himself in a thoughtful manner. "I never knew he had it in him. He looks as if butter wouldn't melt in his mouth."

"It's them books," declared Mrs. Trail, for the books were the cornerstone of the whole affair in her opinion. "It's them 'orrible books what made 'im so strong an' fierce. 'E wouldn't never 'ave 'urt a fly, such a nice quiet young gentleman as 'e always was. I'm goin' to burn them books, every one."

"Ahem," said the Colonel. "Ahem . . . yes . . . well perhaps in a way you're right . . . mustn't let books like that get into the wrong hands, eh? But I think . . . ahem . . . I think I'll just take a couple home with me, Mrs. Trail . . . ahem . . . just to see . . . er . . . to see . . . ahem . . ." He laid half-a-crown on the counter, and gathering up a few of the pamphlets at random he turned and left the shop.

CHAPTER
TWENTY-FOUR

Foiled by Harold in his endeavour to get Jane alone, Charles lost no time in returning to the attack. There had been something in Jane's eyes which had given him a good deal of hope, and at least she liked him, she had said so in plain words. It was an exhilarating feeling to be "liked" by Jane. Next morning Charles and Edgar were early on the well known road to Dingleford Cottage, the former full of deep laid schemes, and carefully prepared speeches for Miss Fortune's undoing. He had decided on a "special place" for his proposal of marriage — a rocky hill near the moor road from whence a fine view could be obtained — and he was determined to lure his victim to this spot, climb the hill with her, and propose marriage on the top. Although practical in some ways Charles was sufficiently old fashioned and sentimental to crave a fine setting for his big scene, and Palmer's Hill was the finest setting he could think of in the neighbourhood. There was also another advantage in choosing Palmer's Hill, and Charles had not overlooked it. You could climb the hill with safety, but not too easily and Jane would certainly require his help when they came to that steep bit near the top. Once he had offered her his hand he could offer to let her keep it for life — she had his heart already.

Charles and Edgar met Miss Fortune at the gate of Dingleford Cottage with her shopping basket on her arm, and this was rather favourable to Charles' plans, for he was able to suggest that he should take her to the village, and "go for a bit of a spin on the way home."

It was such a lovely day that Jane consented; her cold had completely vanished and the drive would do her good. She did her shopping at Mrs. Trail's and then Edgar's nose was turned northwards and away they sped, past Suntrap and out into the country beyond.

"It's a special road," Charles told her, "and it doesn't take very long to do the round. Mother loves this road and so do I — and there's a lovely view from the top of a hill," he added guilefully.

"Do let's see it," said Jane.

"We will," Charles told her. "We'll stop when we get there and climb up." It was all beautifully arranged.

The road ascended onto heathery moors, bright with the morning sun and descended through pine woods shady and fragrant. There was a faint blue haze over the land, promising heat, and the distant hills were but a misty outline against the sky. Edgar was doing well this morning; he bucketed along, grunting a bit on the hills but taking the levels at a good thirty.

"It wouldn't be so nice if we went any faster," Jane pointed out, "because we shouldn't see the country so well."

"But you want to be *able* to go faster?"

194

"If you were able to go faster you'd go," she declared and this was so true that there was no denial possible.

"I like Edgar," Jane continued dreamily. "Edgar's a person. I've liked Edgar tremendously ever since that morning when he spoke to me in the drive."

Charles laughed, but not very heartily, for they were nearing Palmer's Hill and he had begun to sweat gently under the collar at the prospect of the frightful ordeal ahead. Supposing he found, when they got to the top, that he had forgotten all his speeches, or supposing Jane said no. Perhaps I shouldn't ask her yet, thought Charles, wretchedly swithering. Perhaps it's too soon. How long have I known her? It feels like always but it's only really about a month.

Jane noticed his silence but she did not mind, for she was enjoying herself thoroughly. They were high up on the moor now and the bell heather was ablaze with purple-pink blossom.

The road — it was little more than a track — wound in and out of rocky tors, dipping and climbing and curving like a snake.

"This is it," said Charles at last. "That rocky hill on the left is Palmer's Hill. I'll just go round this corner because there's a quarry where I can leave the car —"

He had hardly spoken when a huge black Daimler came round the corner towards them; it was driven by a chauffeur with a fat red face. The car was on the crown of the road, and going fast and Jane thought that a head-on collision was inevitable. She almost screamed, but not quite, for she was a courageous young woman. Fortunately Charles kept his head, he wrenched the steering wheel and swerved onto a grassy stretch at the side of the road. The Daimler sped by without touching them, and Edgar's rear wheels sank up to the hubs in a bog.

"Poggle Wallah!" cried Charles, apostrophising the fat-faced driver as the big car disappeared down the hill in a cloud of dust. "Kabar dar! Ullu kar batcha! Soor kar batcha!"

His face was so furious that Jane had to laugh. "Oh, Charles!" she cried. "That sounded frightful — whatever does it mean?"

"It means — well it means I don't like him much," declared Charles joining in her laughter, for now that he discovered that no great harm was done, and his companion was unhurt and even unalarmed, his good nature reasserted itself.

They had jumped out of the car by this time and were surveying the damage; beyond the fact that Edgar was listing heavily to port and could not be moved without assistance the damage was nil.

"That's good," said Jane. "I shouldn't like poor Edgar to get hurt. We'll just have to wait till somebody comes and meanwhile you can tell me what you *said*."

"What I said?"

"Yes, oolloo something or other — *you* know. Was it frightfully rude, Charles?"

"I know something ruder," said Charles with modest pride.

"It would be awfully useful to know. Say it again, Charles."

"No," said Charles firmly.

196

"Why not?"

"It would be most unsuitable."

"Oolloo — kar — bootcher," she practised, crinkling up her brown eyebrows in her endeavour to remember the words.

"NO!" said Charles again, more firmly than before.

"Oh Charles, why not? Nobody would understand what it meant."

"They would in India."

"But I'm not going to India," she pointed out.

"Oh Jane, you *are!*" he cried, seizing her hand. "I mean you *must*, darling . . . I mean I simply can't go back without you . . . I couldn't bear it . . . I should jump overboard in the Bay. Oh Jane, you simply must come with me . . . you will, won't you . . . it isn't too soon . . ."

"No," said Jane.

"No!" he cried in horrified tones. "Oh Jane, you *must —*"

"I meant '*no it isn't too soon,*'" said Jane laughing tremulously.

Emma Weatherby waited half an hour for her lunch, and then started without Charles, but also without much appetite. It was foolish to be frightened of course, because there was probably some perfectly simple reason for his non-appearance. Edgar might have turned sulky, for instance, as he so often did — but do what she could it was impossible to banish from her mind the horrible list of accidents which appeared every day in the newspapers, and were given out every night by the wireless announcer. There were cars which dashed into each other, with a crash of splintering glass; cars which got out of control and crashed into trees, or telegraph poles or over bridges; cars which, suddenly, and for no apparent reason, burst into flames.

"Emma, you're a fool!" she declared, and helped herself largely to the raspberry flan which she had caused to be prepared for her son's delectation.

She had scarcely done so when her courage was rewarded. She heard Edgar's peculiar grunts, and the scrape of his tyres on the drive, and, a moment after, Charles rushed in full of apologies for his delay.

"We were ditched by a foul red-faced fellow in a Daimler," he explained, "and there we had to remain until somebody else appeared. It was the moor road, near Palmer's Hill. Eventually a man came with a van, an awfully decent chap, and he fixed a rope to Edgar's snout and hauled us onto dry ground. No damage at all."

"Good," said Emma smiling.

"You weren't anxious?"

"Of course not," declared Emma untruthfully.

"Sensible woman!" said Charles, kissing the top of her head.

He sat down at the table and began to eat his lunch, and Emma became aware that there was something very odd the matter with him; indeed it did not require much perspicacity to see it. He hummed to himself below his breath, he laughed suddenly at nothing at all, he used a spoon for his fish. Then he twisted his table

198

napkin into a rag and looked at it as if he had never seen it before and tried to stuff it into his pocket.

"You didn't — you didn't get a bump on the head or anything?" she enquired a trifle anxiously.

"Bump? No, no bump," said Charles. "No bump at all," and he laughed again.

There was silence for a few minutes and then Emma asked him to pass her the butter. She asked him three times before he took the slightest notice of her request and then he looked at her blankly.

"Butter? What butter?"

"Butter," replied Emma patiently, "to spread on my biscuit."

"Oh, *butter!*" he said, smiling at her and passing her the salt.

Emma laughed. "You had better tell me about it," she declared.

"Tell you?"

"Has she said 'yes'?"

"Oh Mother, how on earth did you know — you witch! I was going to tell you after lunch, directly after. I wanted to explain it all so carefully. Darling, you mustn't think I don't love you just as much as ever," said Charles earnestly, "because I do . . . just as much . . . *more* really."

"I know, my dear. It's lovely about Jane . . . I'm so glad."

"It won't make a bit of difference between us," he continued. "Not the least scrap. Only, instead of two of us like there has always been, there will be three of us, you and me and Jane. Jane loves you awfully, she said

199

so, and I'm sure you'll get to like her in time. Don't cry, darling!"

"I'm not," declared Emma, wiping her eyes. "It's because I'm so happy. I love her already Charles, she's a dear."

Charles was hugging her now. "You're not losing me," he assured her.

"It's because I'm happy . . . I can't help crying . . . you know what a fool I am."

"You and I and Jane — three of us," he repeated, trying to mop up her tears with his table-napkin.

"I know . . . Oh Charles, it's lovely! I've been hoping for this to happen."

"You haven't!"

"I have, really."

"Cross your heart?"

"Cross my heart," said Emma earnestly.

"Oh Mother! Then it's perfect . . . it's almost too perfect . . . I'm quite frightened . . ."

"No," said Emma, pulling herself together and shaking her head at him vigorously. "No, you mustn't say that. There's a perfect time in everybody's life — this is yours. Seize it, Charles and be thankful, not frightened. You've found the right woman and there is nothing to keep you apart . . . don't let anything keep you apart . . . go forward bravely."

Emma's tears were dried now, for happy tears are soon forgotten, and presently, after they had discussed Jane's charms and all her endearing qualities to their hearts' content, they began to talk of the future, and to make their plans. Jane had stipulated that the engagement was to be a secret for a week — this was quite a natural demand. Charles had suggested September for the wedding and Jane had said October. Emma Weatherby smiled when she heard this for it was exactly what she would have done herself, she soothed Charles, who was slightly worried, dear simpleton, to think that Jane had chosen a month later than need be for the ceremony, and declared that October was an excellent month. The Italian Lakes would be gorgeous in October.

"Como!" said Charles. "That's an idea!" He sat back and smiled idiotically.

CHAPTER
TWENTY-FIVE

Tea was over at Dingleford Cottage and Nannie was busy washing up the dishes. Joan was sitting on the edge of the kitchen table eating an apple. She had enjoyed herself thoroughly while Jane was ill in bed, but now that Jane was better and going about as usual, she saw that she was in for a dull time. When Jane went out she had to stay at home — and Jane seemed to be out all the time. Joan bit into the apple with her white teeth and considered the matter from various angles.

Nannie, coming in from the scullery, glanced at her sideways and was aware from long experience, that there was mischief in the air. "Now then, Miss Joan, what is it?" she enquired, putting down her tray of crockery with a bang. "I can see you're up to something. I'm not goin' to 'ave no nonsense with the Capting, so there! 'E's Miss Jane's young man."

"I don't want him," said Joan frankly.

"Well, you keep orf 'im, then," said Nannie truculently. "You've got your own young men, Mr. Jack an' all. You leave Miss Jane's young man alone."

"I tell you I don't want him. He bores me."

"Well, what *do* you want? What's the matter with you?"

Joan considered this, munching reflectively. What *was* the matter with her? What was the cause of that vague depression, that restlessness, that horrible feeling that life was flat and stale and not worth living?

"I knows you," Nannie continued. "You're in love, that's what, but if you're thinkin' of monkeyin' about with the Capting it's over my dead body it'll be."

Joan seemed quite unmoved by this remarkable and somewhat gruesome pronouncement. "It's not him at all," she declared.

"Well who is it then?"

"Nobody," said Joan flatly.

She got down off the table and peered out of the window; it was a perfect summer evening, warm and sunny and golden, and here was she, boxed up in the stuffy kitchen with Nannie badgering her to death. "I think I'll go out for a walk," she declared.

"Ho yes, an' what if somebody sees you? You're Miss Jane an' Miss Jane's gorn to the village, to that there Women Ruler's Institution that the Vicar's wife's so set on."

"Women Rulers?"

"Women Rulers," repeated Nannie firmly. "That's what she said. I 'eard 'er with my own ears, but what she wants Women Rulers for . . . Men Rulers are bad enough! Any 'ow she's gorn — Miss Jane I mean — so you just stay where you are. Miss Jane can't be two places at onst."

"Nobody'll see me."

"They better not. The truth is you'd better stop this nonsense, Miss Joan. I don't 'old with all this deceitfulness — never did. If there's any 'anky panky I'll give you away. So now you knows."

"We're going to stop it soon," Joan told her. "We've been talking about it, Nannie. It's difficult, you see. I mean there's so much to explain."

"Get on with it then," said Nannie, unsympathetically.

Joan sighed. The situation was extremely delicate, for the twins had got themselves into a frightful tangle of mistaken identity and they could not agree as to how it was to be resolved. Jane wanted it cleared up at once (for some reason which she had not divulged) but Joan had pleaded so hard for delay that she had been granted three days grace. *Three days*, thought Joan in disgust, it was little enough time in which to straighten out her two knotty problems. The first problem was M. Delaine, of course, and she had written to Jack that morning asking him to find out what the man was doing, and whether he had transferred his affections to some other young woman in Joan's absence. She did not see how Jack was going to accomplish this somewhat delicate mission, but there was always a chance he might. The second problem was Harold. How on earth was she to explain everything to Harold?

It was strange, Joan thought, that number two problem now seemed the bigger and more fearsome. Delaine's image had faded somewhat, while Harold's had become more vivid in her mind. "Life is queer!" said Joan to herself, and then she added fiercely, "Life is . . . is *hellish*, that's what it is," and suddenly she could bear the stuffy kitchen no longer.

Nannie was in the scullery so the coast was clear and Joan escaped by the parlour window and ran down through the devastated area to the new road. It was very quiet and peaceful for the men had stopped work on the bridge and gone home to their suppers. Joan took the opportunity of having a good look at the bridge and she saw that it was nearly finished. It was a concrete structure with two arches, supported in the middle by a concrete pier. The stream was wide here and the banks low and sloping, and the bed of the stream was composed of rock and gravel.

Joan leaned over the edge of the parapet and looked down at the slowly running water. How clear it was, as clear as crystal and the trees on the opposite bank were reflected with faithful accuracy in its calm bosom. She saw a small trout rise to a fly beneath the branches of an overhanging hazel tree and a kingfisher flashed through the arch with a flutter of rainbow wings.

Joan now turned her attention to the road which stretched as far as eye could see in both directions. There was nothing on the road, not even a bicycle, for until the bridge was finished it led nowhere, except of course to Dingleford Cottage. Joan sighed. She decided that the road would look much nicer with a little traffic on it, for silence and isolation did not appeal to her. It would be fun when the bridge was opened and they could erect their notice board and open the tea-room. She climbed onto an iron girder which was sticking up in the air and surveyed the landscape carefully. Was she looking for somebody? Surely not, for had she not given her word to Nannie that nobody would see her? It must be admitted, however, that Joan showed no signs of surprise when she saw a little speck appear, far in the distance, upon the hitherto barren surface of the road. She turned round so that she could watch the speck more easily and, straining her eyes in the vain endeavour to recognise its significance, soon became convinced that it was a man with a dog. Joan shut her eyes and counted up to a hundred very slowly; when she opened them the man was much nearer, so much nearer that there was very little doubt as to his identity. Joan smiled. There was still plenty of time for her to hide; she could either jump down and take refuge behind one of the little huts where the men kept their tools, or she could dodge down into the bushes beside the stream and make her way back to the cottage.

Joan thought about both these courses of action, but took neither. She remained where she was, shutting her eyes again and counting another hundred — slightly faster — and, by the time she had done this, she could hear the ring of footsteps on the road. It was too late to hide now, what a pity! She leant over the edge of the girder and said "Hullo, Harold!"

Harold looked up and their eyes met; a slow flush swept over his face, his mouth opened in astonishment and delight, but no sound came.

"Come up here," said Joan invitingly. "It's lovely . . . such a gorgeous view. I want you to tell me the names of all the hills and things, and which house belongs to who."

Harold had Francesca on a lead today; he tied her to a stanchion and ascended with agility. They sat on the

206

girder side by side and surveyed the scene. It was wide rolling country of fields and pastures made various by old red brick farm houses and copses of fine trees. The course of the Dingle as it wound amongst the hollows could be traced by the willows which lined its banks. Joan enquired about the Dingle; where it had come from and where it was going; and Harold answered as best he could. They talked about streams in general and Joan voiced her eternal wonder as to how streams and rivers could go on flowing all the time.

"You wouldn't think there would be enough water *behind* to keep on all the time," she declared.

Harold saw the point at once. "Springs, I suppose," he said doubtfully.

Joan agreed that it must be springs, and having settled that, she reminded Harold that he had been invited to ascend for the purpose of pointing out all the places of interest in the neighbourhood. Harold complied at once as he would have complied with any request made by Joan. He showed her the church tower, peeping from amongst the trees, and Colonel Staunton's red roof, and the Ames' white cottage designed as a Dutch Homestead.

"What's that house on the very top of the hill?" Joan enquired with interest.

"That's our house, of course, 'Suntrap'," replied Harold. "You've been to Suntrap several times, haven't you?"

Joan did not answer, she saw that it was an opportunity to explain her identity to Harold and she wanted to do it because it had ceased to be any fun to deceive him, but she was frightened. She was so frightened that her throat blocked by an enormous lump. Perhaps he would be disgusted with her . . . perhaps he would not like her any more . . . he would be sure to think that a girl who acted a lie was a despicable creature. Joan had begun by being sorry for Harold and liking him in a half-contemptuous way but that seemed long ago and now she valued his high opinion of her more than she would have owned. I won't say anything yet, thought Joan. She still had three days in which to reveal her deception, and there would be better opportunities later.

Harold did not notice Joan's continued silence, for he was deep in thought; he felt completely happy and comfortable as he always did when he was with Joan. He admired Erica of course, but she made him feel a fool. She was always urging him to "break his shackles" and get a job, and the odd thing was that the more Erica prodded, the less Harold wanted to do. Joan never urged him to do anything, but when he was with her he felt he could conquer the world. This train of thought led very naturally to another:

"Oh I say!" said Harold suddenly. "I say, you know that French chap? Well, he won't bother you any more."

"Oh, Harold! How d'you know? Is he dead?" enquired Joan hopefully.

"No, worse luck!" replied Harold, chuckling to himself. "They wouldn't let me kill him. I believe I would have. I was so angry with the brute."

"Tell me," said Joan with thoroughly awakened interest. "Tell me the whole thing, where you met him and everything."

208

Harold told her. He told the tale very baldly, but the heroic deed shone through the veils of modesty with no uncertain light.

"Harold," she said, looking at him with shining eyes, "Harold, you're like . . . well you're like Sir Galahad or somebody. I never heard anything like it, *never*. I think you're the bravest person that ever lived."

"No, I'm not," declared Harold, blushing furiously.

"You *are*," she cried, "you *are*. Why he's enormous! He might have killed you. He didn't hurt you did he?"

"No," said Harold. "He . . . well he didn't have a chance, really. I mean, I just hit him and he fell down. That was all."

"That was *all!*" cried Joan. "Why it was splendid, it was most frightfully brave . . . it was wonderful."

Harold was pleased at this praise, but he was also slightly embarrassed. "Widgett says he won't come back," he declared, changing the subject slightly, "and Widgett knows about those sort of things. I don't think he will, either," added Harold reminiscently.

They talked about the heroic deed a bit longer for Joan was anxious to know every smallest detail, and it was not until she was satisfied that there was no more to be told that she remembered the time.

"I must go," said Joan, looking at her watch in dismay. "Nannie will be furious —"

Harold sighed. He could have sat here for hours talking to Joan, but Joan was not the only one who would be expected home. Even if he went now, this instant, he would be late, and must invent some plausible excuse to appease his mother's curiosity. And, for another thing, Francesca would be getting cold sitting down below, tied to that stanchion. It was a miracle that she had remained there so long without a sound, for she was by no means a patient animal.

They climbed down, Harold helping his companion with quite unnecessary solicitude and soon were standing on the ground.

"Oh!" cried Harold in dismay. "Oh Heavens! Where is Francesca?"

"Who?"

"Francesca. Oh my goodness, she's gone! What *shall* I do?"

Jane perceived the piece of crimson leather still tied securely to the iron bar. It was quite a short piece of leather and the end of it had been chewed through. She saw at once what had happened but it seemed to her that Harold's dismay was excessive.

"Surely it will find its own way home?" she observed.

"It isn't that," declared Harold. "It's because —" he stopped and blushed. Joan was not a "doggy girl", and even if she had been it would have been difficult to explain. Besides, the thought that, even at this moment, Francesca might be making a disastrous *mésalliance*, and of his mother's fury when she discovered it, deprived him of the power of speech. He stood and gaped at Joan like a pink cod-fish, if such a thing can be imagined.

"What *is* the matter, Harold?" Joan enquired.

"It's . . . it's frightful," he cried, almost wringing his hands. "You don't understand, but it *is* frightful. Mother will be simply frantic . . . I've got to find her

". . . and how can I possible find her when I don't know where she has gone?"

"Whistle," suggested Joan, who was aware that properly brought up dogs came when you whistled.

"It wouldn't be the slightest use. Francesca *never* comes when you whistle; besides, by this time, she's probably *miles* away. She may have gone to the village," he added, shuddering at the idea, "or she may have gone to the Manley's gardener's cottage, which would be almost worse. Oh Heavens, whatever shall I do!"

"You had better go and see, I suppose," said Joan crossly. She was annoyed because it seemed to her that Harold was making a ridiculous fuss about the dog. They had had such a nice chat together and now it was all spoilt. Harold was not thinking about her any more, he was thinking about Francesca. Joan was not jealous, of course, for how could you possibly be jealous of a dog, and a horrible fat ugly dog at that? She was just annoyed with Harold for being so silly. "Go and see where the dog's gone, go and look all over Dingleford," she added, waving her hand to the different points of the compass where Francesca might be found, and with that she turned her back on Harold and walked away.

Harold hesitated for a moment and then rushed after her and seized her by the arm.

"Joan!" he cried. "Joan, you musn't be angry with me . . . I told you I was a fool . . . it doesn't matter about Francesca, she can go to hell for all I care . . . Joan, don't be angry with me because I simply can't *bear* it . . . honestly I can't . . . Joan *darling* . . ."

211

CHAPTER
TWENTY-SIX

It was very late indeed when Harold got home, and Francesca was not to blame. In fact Harold had forgotten all about Francesca until he found her waiting for him on the drive outside the front door. He looked at her and wondered vaguely where she had been, but his mind was so taken up with more important matters that Francesca's doings seemed of small account. They went in together and found Mrs. Prestcott in the drawing-room. She had obviously finished dinner at the usual time for the coffee tray stood beside her on the table, and Harold saw that she was engaged in mending his socks. This was a very bad sign for it meant that she was wounded to the core, and a wounded tigress is never a very pleasant animal to encounter. At any other time Harold would have been frightened, but tonight he was so uplifted by happiness, so dazed with joy, that Mrs. Prestcott's anger could not touch him.

"Harold, oh Harold!" cried his Mother in tremulous tones.

"Sorry Mother," Harold said vaguely. "Awfully sorry . . . awfully late, I know . . . couldn't help it . . . awfully sorry really."

212

"It is most inconsiderate," declared Mrs. Prestcott. "I'm surprised at you. The idea of coming home at this hour and expecting dinner to be kept for you. Do you think the servants have nothing to do but to —"

"Dinner! I don't want any dinner."

"Have you had dinner?"

"No, I don't think so . . . No, I haven't, but I'm not hungry."

"I've been nearly mad with worry. You never thought of that, I suppose."

"No . . . I mean I couldn't help it."

"You couldn't *help* it!" she cried. "What *have* you been doing? Do you know that there's a most extraordinary story going about Dingleford? A story to the effect that you attacked and killed a man in the bar-room at the Cat and Fiddle?"

"No, is there?" said Harold vaguely.

"Is it true?" enquired Mrs. Prestcott. She was perfectly certain that it was not true, of course, and had told Colonel Staunton when he called to see her about it that the whole thing was completely without foundation, but she wanted to annoy Harold and rouse him out of his apathy.

Harold tried to collect his thoughts. "I didn't kill the man," he said slowly. "I mean the fellow got up and went off under his own steam."

Mrs. Prestcott gazed at her son in amazement. "Harold, I can't believe it! What were you doing in that horrible place? What on earth has happened to you lately? You're not like yourself at all . . . Harold, you're not attending to me, answer my questions properly."

"What questions?" he enquired.

Mrs. Prestcott had half a dozen questions that required answers, she turned them over hastily and picked upon the one which seemed most urgent. "What have you been doing tonight?" she demanded in firm tones.

"Oh, tonight?" said Harold. "I just walked down to the bridge. I was talking to somebody and I forgot the time."

Mrs. Prestcott's annoyance was giving way to bewilderment. She could not understand Harold's attitude at all. He was usually so docile, so easily amenable, so anxious to propitiate her if she were vexed or annoyed, but tonight he did not seem to notice her vexation or, if he noticed it, did not seem mind. Mrs. Prestcott stared at him with her dark eyes, probing him, trying to find a clue to his strange mood, wondering what to say next, what line to take to bring Harold to his senses.

At this moment the telephone bell rang.

The instrument stood on a table at Mrs. Prestcott's elbow; she lifted the receiver and put it to her ear. "Yes," she said. "Yes . . . who? . . . No, this is Mrs. Prestcott."

"Is it for me?" enquired Harold anxiously. He thought he knew who the caller was, for his mind was completely full of one person at the moment, and, although he had parted from this person barely half an hour ago, he was already sick for the sound of her voice. "Is it for me?" he repeated, trying to take the receiver from his mother's hand.

214

She waved him away. "I will take the message," she said firmly. The observation was really intended for the individual at the other end of the wire, but it did for Harold also, and Harold was so accustomed to her highhandedness that it never occurred to him to dispute her right to take his call. He was not even very much annoyed about it, only disappointed, as a child might have been, and he sat down opposite to his mother and waited as patiently as he could.

The message did not take long to deliver, and the receiver was replaced.

"I don't understand it," said Mrs. Prestcott hopelessly.

"Perhaps I should," suggested Harold.

"It was a Mr. Widgett," she told him. "He seemed rather excited, but I gathered that 'Fair Beauty was O.K.' He said you would understand. Now Harold what does —"

"Oh!" cried Harold, leaping to his feet. "Oh, marvellous! It's *won* . . . I knew it would. Hurrah, this is my lucky day!"

"Harold . . . *Harold*, contain yourself! Are you mad? You've been betting — betting with Widgett, that dreadful man at the inn — *that's* what you were doing at the Cat and Fiddle, I see it all now. Oh Harold, how could you demean yourself . . . I thought you were aware of my views . . ."

"Yes, yes I have," he cried. It was no use to deny the impeachment and indeed he was so elated by his success that he did not want to deny it. "Yes, I've been betting and I've won. Hurrah, I've won *four hundred pounds!*"

Mrs. Prestcott was so taken aback by the magnitude of his winnings that she was temporarily dumb.

"Oh, isn't it splendid!" cried Harold, who was beside himself with delight. "Isn't it marvellous! Four hundred pounds . . . I shall go up to town tomorrow and buy her a ring . . . diamonds, of course . . . all girls love diamonds . . . perhaps a yellow diamond . . . a huge one . . ."

He was unaware that he was speaking his thoughts aloud, for two marvellous pieces of luck in as many hours had made him quite drunk with success. His win on the horse was a small matter, of course, compared with his other victory, but a small whisky on the top of several large ones is often the undoing of a man. In Harold's case it had changed his mood from dazed, half incredulous bliss to wild and voluble excitement. He was walking about the room by this time, waving his arms and declaring that he would buy the biggest diamond Hatton Garden could produce for the dearest girl in the world. Fair Beauty's money should purchase Fair Beauty's ring, what could be fitter . . .

Mrs. Prestcott found her voice. "Sit down at once, Harold," she screamed. "Are you drunk or crazy? Have you no consideration for your mother?"

Harold's stride faltered and the fire died out of his eyes.

"What does this mean?" she asked, following up her advantage. "Do you hear me? Harold, what does this mean? Sit down at once and tell me what you have

216

done. It's that Fortune girl, that horrible detestable creature . . . I wish I had never laid eyes on her . . . sit *down*, Harold!"

Harold sat down. All of a sudden he was completely sober. He felt weak and empty and quite unfit for the frightful scene which he saw approaching.

"I'm waiting," said Mrs. Prestcott in awesome tones. "I'm waiting, Harold. I think I have a right to know what all this means."

He saw that she had this right. He had rights too, but he could not see them so clearly. There was not very much to tell, and Sylvia Prestcott had guessed the whole thing already. She had seen the danger that dreadful night at the dance, and had done her best to avert it, but she made Harold tell her just the same. Harold blundered through his story, and with every word his courage ebbed away, as Sylvia had foreseen. His love for Joan, and the almost incredible fact that she returned his love, had seemed a splendid thing, brave and shining and beautiful, but now it had lost its glory and was muddied and obscured. Sylvia Prestcott turned it over and showed him another side: she had given up her whole life for him, and he was proposing to throw her over for a girl he scarcely knew. Did he think the girl would stick to him? Did he think that any girl would be contented to live with him for ever? She would soon tire of him, Sylvia declared.

"She said she loved me," said Harold wretchedly.

"And what about *me?*" Sylvia raged. "Don't I love you? Haven't I given up everything for you, and slaved for you all my life? Is this how you show your gratitude for all that I've given up, for all my years of care and devotion? You go off, without saying a word and become engaged to a girl you know nothing about. I could tell you something about her if I chose to lower myself. She's a dreadful creature, utterly impossible. You could never be happy with a girl like that. You needn't think she loves you at all — it's your money she's after. She wants to marry you because she thinks you're well off and could give her a good time. She's fooled you, Harold, she's fooled you!"

It was a frightful scene, a thousand times worse than any 'scene' Harold could remember. He felt quite dazed with the violence of her rage. It's hopeless, he thought, quite hopeless . . . I could never go through with it . . . I couldn't ask Joan to go through with it either . . . and perhaps mother's right . . . perhaps I'm too much of a worm . . . what girl could go on loving a worm?

CHAPTER
TWENTY-SEVEN

The extremes of bliss and misery demand the same alleviation of the restlessness which they induce. Thus Charles, who was mad with joy at the rosy future which he envisaged, and Harold, who was utterly wretched at the destruction of his hope, conceived the same idea at almost the same moment, and decided to go for a long walk in the dark. The moor road was a natural choice, for it was long and lonely, and thither the blissful Charles turned his steps; he was passing Suntrap when Harold reached the gate, and the two young men met face to face.

"Charles!" Harold exclaimed in surprise. "Where are you off to?"

"I'm going for a walk — long walk," Charles declared.

"May I . . . would you mind if I came too?" enquired Harold diffidently.

Charles did not really want a companion, for his thoughts of Jane were companions enough, but he was in such a benignant state of mind that refusal was impossible.

"Come on, then," he said, quite amiably, "but you'll have to step out. I'm in the mood for stepping out tonight."

"Right," agreed Harold. "It's the moor road, I suppose."

They stepped out together, northwards, into the open country which lay beyond Suntrap and, as they strode along, the years which had made a barrier between them seemed to dwindle away. This road was familiar to them both, though it was years since they had trodden it together, and by the time they were half way across the moor they were boys again, boon companions as they had always been.

It really was a beautiful night for a walk. The moon was full and very bright; it shone low down in the sky like a silver disk making the whole world black and silver. The trees' shadows were like velvet on the ground, and the shadows of the two men stretched before them, moving silently over the narrow road. On either side was the moor clad with heather and broken by clumps of fir trees and pines and an occasional pile of boulders. The sky itself was deep dark blue, and a few small clouds moved slowly across its surface, driven by the light breeze.

Charles and Harold strode on. At first they spoke little, and only of impersonal matters or of memories shared.

"Remember that stunted tree?" Charles enquired.

"Rather, there was a hedge-sparrow's nest in it, wasn't there?"

"Mphn," said Charles.

"There's the rock where we had our fire," said Harold suddenly. "Seems smaller somehow, don't you think."

220

"Yes, by Jove! I always thought it was a huge sort of rock. You fell off the top of it one day — remember that?"

Of course Harold remembered.

"I thought you were dead," Charles declared.

Harold had thought he was dead too, or very nearly. He remembered that for a few minutes he had been numb all over, no feeling at all in his limbs, and then there had been a queer sensation of pins and needles and he had been very sick. Queer how these things came back to one.

"Heavens, what a funk I was in!" added Charles, laughing reminiscently. "I can remember it well."

It was very pleasant to recall the old days, but after a bit Harold's misery returned and he felt the urge to consult Charles about his troubles. It was no new thing for him to take his troubles to Charles. Charles was so splendid, so completely unafraid, so clear-sighted. Was it possible that Charles could find some sort of solution to the problem?

"I'm in an awful mess, Charles," he said at last.

"What sort of a mess?" enquired his friend sympathetically.

"It's mother," Harold began, and Charles could not help smiling, for Harold's tales of woe had always begun in exactly the same way. "It's Mother. You know I've always done what she wanted, *always*, but now there's something I want to do . . . something that means everything to me . . . and I can't . . . I can't escape," cried Harold wildly. "It's too late, or something . . . she's *got* me, Charles."

"Nonsense, of course you can escape if you want to," Charles told him soothingly.

"It's a girl," declared Harold, in a burst of confidence. "The one and only girl in the world. I never cared much for girls, but now . . . Oh Charles, I *can't* give her up."

"Why should you?"

"Mother," said Harold simply.

Charles was silent for a moment or two. The position was perfectly clear to him for he knew Mrs. Prestcott. The girl was Erica, of course, but there was no need to mention names; he could help Harold without that.

"It's *your* life," he said at last. "She has absolutely no right to interfere. Stand on your own feet, Harold."

"I've tried to," said Harold miserably, "but I haven't *got* any feet. I hate rows so frightfully . . . I can't bear scenes . . . they make me feel sick and then I'm done. I open my mouth to speak and no sound comes out — it's ghastly. And then there's another thing; have I any right to marry a girl when I'm such a grovelling coward?"

"You aren't a coward," cried Charles. "Good heavens, man, look at the way you knocked down that fellow in Widgett's bar! That great enormous hulk! I'd have thought twice before tackling the fellow myself!"

"That's quite different," explained Harold. "It's moral courage I need. You don't know what a worm I am; I can't even — she doesn't let me choose my own clothes."

They walked on for a little while in silence; it was certainly a very serious problem.

"Look here!" said Charles at last. "There's only one way — take a firm line. Don't say any more but just go and get married to . . . to the girl. She's sporting enough," he continued, thinking of Erica of course, "and she knows how things are. Go up to town and get married. You can get a special licence or something — I'll help you."

"Charles!" cried Harold. He had hoped for bold advice, and by Heaven he had got it.

"Well, why not?"

"Mother would — Mother would *die*."

Charles did not think that anything so desirable would occur. "She'd probably give in when she found that the deed was done," he said wisely.

"Would it be right?"

"Right?"

"I mean she's my mother. She has given up everything for me."

"No she hasn't," said Charles firmly. "She hasn't given up anything for you. She's selfish. No mother has a right to . . . to swallow her children whole."

Harold digested this. He admired Charles so profoundly that he was ready to believe all he said, and it was true — yes, every word of it was true. He felt a strange uplifting of the spirit, almost as if a burden had fallen off his back.

"Then I needn't be grateful to her any more!" he cried. This was the strangest thing he had said yet, or so Charles thought, for surely gratitude is not a duty to be demanded but rather a feeling or quality which like mercy falls from Heaven like gentle rain; and, still like mercy, "blesseth him that gives and him that takes".

"Oh Charles!" continued Harold. "It *is* the only way. I shall ask her to do it. I shall ask her to marry me now instead of November as we arranged, and we'll go up to town and get married without telling a soul."

"Good man!" exclaimed his friend, delighted at the success of his bold advice. "Good man! That's the spirit! You've found the girl you want — don't let anything come between you." He had a vague feeling as he uttered the words that he had heard them before; they seemed to ring in his ears with a familiar sound, but he had no time to think of that now. "There's a perfect time in everybody's life," he continued. "This is yours, seize it. Don't let anything keep you apart; go forward bravely."

"Yes," said Harold, who thought it sounded splendid.

"You've got the girl to think of too," Charles pointed out. "You can't let her down, old man. She loves you, I suppose?"

"Yes," said Harold. He was quite sure of that apparently. "Yes, the whole thing was settled this afternoon. I mean we talked it over and it all seemed . . . seemed splendid, until Mother . . . but it's clear again now, thanks to you, old fellow. I've got a small income of my own so I'm independent of Mother in that way, and of course I mean to get a job, any sort of a job."

"I'll help you," Charles promised. "I'll find out about the special licence and that. All you've got to do is to get hold of Erica and fix it up with her. She'll be on for it if I know her," declared Charles. "It's just the sort of thing —"

"Erica!" cried Harold, "but Charles, old thing, it isn't Erica at all." He laughed excitedly. "I mean I like Erica most awfully as a friend, but, to tell you the truth, she frightens me rather. Fancy your thinking it was Erica! . . . I must tell you," he continued confidentially, "I've told you so much already, and I know she wouldn't mind me telling *you*. I mean she *did* say it was to be a secret for a bit, but I know you're as safe as the bank . . . It's J — Jane."

"Jane!" cried Charles, stopping dead in his tracks and looking at his friend incredulously. "Jane Fortune?"

"Yes, Jane. Are you surprised? Of course you are. I know I'm not nearly good enough for her," said Harold humbly.

"I *am* surprised," said Charles in a queer hard voice. "You see Jane Fortune did me the honour . . . she said..I mean I asked her to marry me this afternoon and she accepted me."

"But Charles!" cried Harold in consternation.

"It's funny, isn't it?" said Charles with a forced laugh.

"But Charles . . . I mean it was all *settled*."

"That's what I thought."

"We were to be married in November —"

"October was the month she chose for *our* wedding."

"But she can't . . . she can't marry both of us!"

"One wouldn't have thought so."

"I suppose there can't be any *mistake*," said Harold. "I mean of course any girl would rather . . . well, I mean any girl would be bound to like you best —"

"Shut up, Harold," said Charles firmly. "We shan't get anywhere if you start that nonsense. We've got to face the thing squarely."

"Yes," said Harold.

"We've got to get to the bottom of it."

"Yes."

"Be perfectly open with each other."

"Yes, of course."

"Well then: when you asked her to marry you what did she say?"

Harold thought hard. "I don't remember," he declared. "Honestly Charles, I can't remember what she said, but . . . well . . . somehow or other I found myself . . . er . . . kissing her, you know . . . and she . . . she seemed to like it," added Harold miserably.

Charles let fly with his stick at an unoffending bush which stood by the roadside, and a stream of quite unprintable language issued from his lips.

"Yes," said Harold, in a relieved tone. "Yes, go on Charles, that's exactly how I feel."

"There's only one thing to be done," said Charles when he had come to the end of his vocabulary. "Only one thing. Come on, Harold."

He turned slap round and strode back towards Dingleford with Harold at his heels.

CHAPTER
TWENTY-EIGHT

The two Miss Fortunes were rather above themselves tonight. Nannie had a dreadful time trying to chase them to bed. They had undressed at the right time as good as gold, and had come down to the parlour as usual to drink their milk, but now it was half past ten — high time they were in bed — and Nannie had been in twice already to tell them so.

"There's somethin' up," she declared, "some mischief or other — don't I know it!"

Joan chuckled engagingly.

"What's it all about?" enquired Nannie. "Where's the joke? What 'ave you two been up to? You've been sittin' there talkin' for hours, an' you're not through yet seemingly. It's a wonder to me what you two finds to talk about."

"You'd be surprised," declared Joan.

"Nothin' wouldn't surprise me where you're concerned," Nannie told her. "It's somethin' to do with that trick you're playin' pretendin' to be each other. You're too old for that nonsense now, an' there'll be trouble come of it, mark my words. Such carryin's-on I never saw. What 'ave you been doing, eh?"

"Wouldn't you like to know?" Joan enquired, cheekily.

Jane shook her head at her irrepressible twin; it was bad policy to get Nannie all worked up like this. She might refuse to give them their supper in the parlour tomorrow night or put them on a diet of stewed steak and milk pudding for days.

Joan caught the signal out of the corner of her eye and realised the danger immediately. "Nannie dear," she said, looking all of a sudden as if butter wouldn't melt in her mouth. "Nannie dear, I *will* be good *really*. I'm excited, that's all, and you know how I always get when I'm excited, don't you. Tell us a story, Nannie — just one before we go up to bed. Tell us about the day we were born — you know the one."

"You've 'eard it I don'-know-'ow-many times," declared Nannie roundly. "It's just a wheeze to put off time, that's what. I knows you, Miss Joan."

"Oh Nannie, you haven't told us about it for *ever* so long," Jane cried. "It's one of your very best stories, too."

"Oh well," said Nannie, in a relenting sort of voice. "Oh well . . . but you must go up directly after —"

They nodded solemnly.

Nannie smiled, she loved a good yarn herself, and was by no means displeased at the twins' eagerness to hear her tell it.

"Well," she began, "Well, *there* was the pore major sittin' in the lib'ry, an' there was I poppin' in an' out to look at 'im. They didn't want me upstairs for that there nurse — all starched an' stiff she was — shooed me off

228

every time I put my 'ead above the bannisters. Well, *there* was the major sittin' or walkin' about with 'is pipe smokin' like a factory, an' there was me tryin' to get 'im to 'ave a cup o' tea; an' then, suddenly, in walks the nurse with a proud kind of smile as if she 'ad done somethin' clever — which she 'adn't at all, for she wasn't a wonder at the best of times. 'It's two little girls,' she says to the major, smilin' in a proud kind of way. 'There now, two dear little girls. Isn't that lovely?'

" 'What!' cries the major, droppin' 'is pipe in the grate where it smashed the end off. 'What did you say, woman?'

" 'Two dear little girls,' says the nurse again, as proud as punch. 'An' all goin' well.'

"The Major looks at 'er in a queer kind of way. ' 'Oly Moses!' 'e says. ' 'Oly Moses, I might 'ave known there'd be two.'

" 'And 'ow might you 'ave known?' she says, took aback with surprise.

" 'Because Miss Fortunes never come singly, you fool,' says the pore gentleman."

The twins laughed uproariously, just as if they had never heard the story before.

"Oh Nannie, it's a lovely story," cried Joan.

"I had forgotten how funny it was," added Jane chuckling. "Poor Daddy, it *was* rather awful for him wasn't it."

" 'E was a bit fed up at first," Nannie agreed, " 'im wantin' a son so bad to go to Sand'urst an' what not, but you weren't three days old but what 'e was as proud of you both as any peacock, an' that's a fact. An' 'e always *was* proud of you, an' fond too," added Nannie earnestly, "so don't you forget it."

At this moment the front door bell rang, it rang with no ordinary sound, but with a long and violent commotion which set the wretched wires vibrating all over the house.

"That's torn it," exclaimed Nannie inelegantly. "It's gone for good this time I shouldn't wonder. Drat that bell! Now 'oo on earth can it be at this time of night ... my goodness, look at the time ... a quarter to eleven ... 'oo on earth?" She bustled away muttering to herself and left the twins in the parlour.

It was certainly very late for callers at Dingleford Cottage, and Nannie was careful to open the door no more than a crack till she saw who the visitor might be. She peered out through the crack and saw two gentlemen standing on the doorstep, and the moon was bright enough to show that the two gentlemen were none other than Mr. Prestcott and Captain Weatherby.

"Ha!" exclaimed Nannie in an 'I told you so' kind of way.

"Nannie," said Charles, in a low earnest tone. "Nannie, I know it seems an extraordinary time to call, but we had to come. There's something ... I mean we simply must see Miss Fortune *now*. She isn't in bed, is she?"

"No, she ain't," said Nannie grimly. "She ought to be, but she ain't, an' you shall see 'er — Ho, yes you shall! Both of you shall see 'er before you're any older. I jes' thought it would come to this," she added, ushering them into the hall and taking their hats and sticks from their unresisting hands. "I thought there was mischief brewing, an' I wasn't wrong — my words 'as come true, that's what."

"It's just . . . just s-something we w-want to ask her," stammered Harold, who had been dragged into this astonishing adventure by his intrepid companion.

"You *shall* ask 'er," Nannie declared. "I said you should, an' you shall. I've 'ad enough of this nonsense . . . a joke's a joke, but some people doesn't know where to stop . . . Walk in please." And so saying she threw open the door of the parlour and almost pushed them in.

The room was lamp-lit with a soft rosy glow, and very pleasant and cosy it seemed. There was a little table in the middle of the floor with a plate of cakes upon it and two empty tumblers which had once contained milk. On the sofa, which faced the door, sat the two Miss Fortunes, clad in pyjamas, and blue silk dressing gowns. They were sitting one at each end of the sofa, half facing each other, with their legs tucked under them in exactly the same way and were busily engaged in talking to each other, for even yet their insatiable lust for each other's conversation was not appeased. When the door opened, and Charles and Harold walked in, their two golden heads turned with one accord, their eyes opened widely — their mouths also — and the same expression of incredulous horror appeared upon both their faces.

For nearly twenty seconds the four young people gazed at each other without a sound, and then Joan began to laugh. Jane had to laugh too — how could she help it? And Charles and Harold, after struggling for a moment to look suitably dignified and stern, abandoned the hopeless attempt and joined in the merriment with manly roars.

They laughed and laughed, but despite the extravagance of their mirth, it was observed and noted with satisfaction by each Miss Fortune that her particular swain was in no doubt as to the identity of his own. Love who is proverbially blind was not blind to the different personalities of Joan and Jane. Charles kept his eyes firmly fixed upon Jane, with only an occasional glance at Joan to make comparisons and to decide finally that they were alike of course, but that Jane was really a thousand times more adorable and dear; while Harold, by exactly the same method arrived at the opposite conclusion.

"Oh dear!" cried Joan rocking herself to and fro. "Oh dear . . . your faces!"

"Can you wonder?" Harold gasped. "Good Heavens, the shock might have killed us!"

"You little devils!" exclaimed Charles, trying to look severe. "You little devils. Oh Jane, how could you?"

"Charles!" said Jane. "Oh Charles, you're not *really* angry, are you?"

"*Don't* be cross with us, Harold," said Joan.

"We can explain *everything*," they added in chorus.

"You'd better," said Charles, with a twinkle in his eye. "I never heard of such a disgraceful thing. It's not decent to be so alike, is it Harold?"

"It explains everything, of course," said Harold feebly, taking out his handkerchief and mopping up his

232

laughter-tears. "I thought of all sorts of explanations, but none of them fitted, I never thought of this. Everything's all right, then —"

"Yes," said Charles. "There's one each."

Also available in ISIS Large Print:

Love or Duty

Roberta Grieve

Louise Charlton sees herself as plain and uninteresting beside her vibrant sister Sarah, a talented singer. When she falls in love with young Doctor Andrew Tate she is convinced he is not interested in her. While Sarah sails to America to pursue her musical career, Louise stays at home, duty-bound to care for her selfish manipulative stepmother. Tricked into marrying James, the son of her father's business partner, she tries to forget Andrew and make the best of things. When James reveals his true nature, Louise throws herself into war work to take her mind off her situation. Her life becomes constrained by duty. Then she meets the young doctor again . . . will love win out over duty for Louise?

ISBN 978-0-7531-8940-5 (hb)
ISBN 978-0-7531-8941-2 (pb)

Alice's Girls

Julia Stoneham

In the last months of World War II, ten Land Girls are serving at Post Stone Farm, under the watchful eye of their warden, Alice Todd. The local Land Army representative had at first been reluctant to give Alice the warden's job, and Roger Bayliss, the farm's owner seemed not to have any confidence in her at all. But she proved herself more than capable of the job and she has won the girls' admiration.

But Alice privately admits that one of the reasons she is so involved with the lives of her girls is that she has worries of her own. Recently divorced and with a ten year-old son to bring up, she fears for the future. When peace is finally declared, and all Alice's girls make plans for their lives after the Land Army, she too has a decision to make.

ISBN 978-0-7531-8836-1 (hb)
ISBN 978-0-7531-8837-8 (pb)